MS. PULCHRITUDINOUS

MS. PULCHRITUDINOUS

The Commanding Chief of the U.S.A.

Bobby R. Wilson

Ordering Information:

For orders and inquiries, please contact:
1-888-404-1388
www.goldtouchpress.com
book.orders@goldtouchpress.com

Printed in the United States of America

Contents

Foreword

This book consists of a group of poems about a beautiful lady, and how she invaded the authors of this book dream, fictionalizing his lifestyle, about meeting her in reality, serving as his lawyer, defending him as a victim of plagiarism, in a retaliating way, such victory caused her popularity to grow with political force, that when they got engaged.

She became the district attorney, before marrying this author, then she sought and won the U.S. Senator's seat with her political convincing ability, later she became governor of that state. Her job was done so great, until she was nominated to be the president of the United States.

Eventually, she got the chance to preside over this nation, with her husband, the author serving as the first gentleman of this nation. After trying to set this world straight with international equality, Earth was attacked by an existence from out of space, and the first man of the United States was assassinated, trying to save the life of his wife, while she was addressing United Earth, preparing the world for a war that was declared on her.

The author dedicates this book of poems and story to all the ladies of this world with Miss Pulchritudinous characteristic, being intellectually attractive with enough smart and heart to be the boss of us all. Such a lady as this, invaded the author's dream, motivated him to write a book about her existence. This story also tells how the imagination of a writer can be used to entertain the existence of other people.

Miss Pulchritudinous
My Valentine Princess

The most beautiful creature
I have ever seen
Was this female human being
Irresistibly eyes pleasing to see

Was her pulchritudinous appearance
Invaded my dream
On February the fourteenth
As though she existed in reality

She came that Valentine's night
Floating through the ceiling of my bedroom
Looking like an angel in flight
Filling my eyes with pure delight

Her articulated skill
Brought pleasure to my ears
Warming my heart
With her captivating voice

She came near my bed
As I lay there halfway scare
Staring at such beautiful sight
I was too amazed to be afraid

As her wings folded back
I felt more relaxed
The sight of her nude appearance
Looked like clear water to me

As she got closer
Her body became more colorful
She had a face of an angel
And a body of a goddess

She stood at a height
Any man will like
Five feet seven inches
With a body's figure

Most women will envy
With a body weight
Other women will appreciate
Their bodies looking this great

By such definition
Miss Pulchritudinous is the description
Of her physical characteristic
Her cute face dazzled me

With such enchanting appearance
Advertising her beautiful eyes
Clear, round, sexy and dreamy
Bright bluish green in color with honey-brown trimming

The length and style of her hair
Brought drama to the clothes
That she wears
Fitting her body with eyes pleasing quality

Her glowingly smooth complexion
Was a blessing to her health
She was more stimulating to see
While wearing a dress

Her nationality did not
Present itself to me
Borne of mixed ethnicity
She was one good-looking lady to see

The fullness of breasts
Stood erected from her chest
What made this lady looked so fine
Was her flat, sexy stomach

Collaborating with her slim waistline
Then she turned around
I saw the world most beautiful behind
Extending outward and curving 'round

Into a stimulating figure
Of a salaciously fine upside
Down heart of Valentine
With deep curving butt cheeks

Connecting to the thighs
Of the world's most gorgeous-looking legs
Splendidly developed, long, healthy and sexy
It would be like heaven

For my eyes to see them spread
Just as that thought entered my mind
She bent over
To pick up something from the floor

Her legs were slightly opened
And what I saw
Would have made a dumb man talk
It brought water to my mouth

She repositioned herself
As she began to climb
Softly into my bed
Her personal hygiene

Was nose-pleasingly clean
Smelling fresh and sweet
To me in this dream
She cuddled up cozy to me

Speaking ears pleasingly
Her polite articulated skill
Brought erection-causing
Pleasure to my ears

She spoke convincingly
That our relationship
Was meant to be
Then she started kissing me

I obliged her overwhelmingly
What a foreplay technique
We were having fun
Manipulating each other's tongue

I began to taste
Her ears, neck, and breasts
Getting her ready for my erection
Then we began to indulge

Into the intimacy of making love
She fit me like a warm, wet
Stretching glove of flesh
What would this world be without sex

She began to moan into my ear
Telling me that her love is sincere
I increased my copulation
Between her thighs

We both witnessed
The thrill of life
This orgasm was so intensified
I damn near passed out

Then she began to fade away
Causing me to awake
Lying in my bed
Alone, wet, and frustrated

She seem so real
Making love to me in that dream
Back to reality
This is the lady for me

If I become successful
I will call it a blessing
Fulfilling my desire
With her as my wife

Motivated by a Dream

I was away from home
As lonely as I could be
I was so bored

Until my mind began
To play tricks on me
Filling my life with misery

I was an unemployed man
With enough skill
To do just about anything

No job is no joy
Life like this
Can be hard to exist

An education without an occupation
Can be very frustrating
Having skill without work experience

Is a legal way to discriminate
The thought of being alone
With no woman to call my own

No one to comfort me
Caused my heart to bleed
Emotionally

Who wants to exist like this
When it comes to the appearance of women
I had eyes of a womanizer

I seem to analyze
Their physical characteristics
Their faces and bodies caught my attention

From my past experience
The women 1 have met
Were unsavory and hungry for sex

They were unable to assist me
With economic help
A retrospective vision

Came to my attention
All the women
I had pleased

Not a one
Was here with me
On February the fourteenth

I was so lonesome
In my bedroom
On this Valentine's night

Until I began to cry
Without a tear
Falling from my eyes

This thoughtful feeling
Was hurting me
Until I fell into a deep sleep

Meeting a young lady
Exquisite to see
With a cute face

And a salacious body figure
She introduced herself to me
As Miss Pulchritudinous

Throughout this dream
She enhanced my existence
With moments of divine

What I experienced with her
Strengthened my mind
Encouraged me to spend some time

Writing a story
With a group of poems
That read like a love song

Describing how the thought
Of this beautiful woman
Made me strong

The Lady of My Dream

I'm known as Bobby Ray, a veteran of the U.S. Navy, with a college education. I was in the navy during the Viet Nam situation. I wanted more prestige than what being an enlisted personnel could receive, so I enrolled into college for intellectual knowledge, four years later I graduated with a B.A. degree in the field of Journalism-Advertising, and ever since the day I graduated. I was faced with a jobless situation. No matter how much effort I put forward of getting hired, a job for me was denied, so I matriculated into a business college to learn word processing, in order to enhance my writing knowledge, and that did not help me in receiving an occupation.

This happened to me in my home state Louisiana. For several years, I was a jobless victim, suffering under an economic depression named after the president of the United States, during his inauguration "Reaganomic." I tried to seek political help, but all I received were statements expressing their regrets. The affirmative action statements on those work applications seem to be a legal way to discriminate.

There I was a black man with a college education, and I had no job to participate. I was fighting off the urge to sell illegal drugs. No matter what type of job I was seeking, I was either over qualified for the position I applied or I was lacking the work experience for the position requiring the education. I took Civil Service tests for different levels of the government: local, parish, state and federal whether I pass or fail, a job for me wasn't there.

I continue seeking the assistant of different politicians. No matter what ethnicity they represented, they were unable to help me. I was finding out the hard way, education doesn't always pay, right then and there; it's not always what you know, but who you know to get your foot into the door of an occupation these days. This economic trouble caused me to move back home with my mother.

There were conflicts between certain family members and me. They seem to envy the success I achieved, by earning a college degree. Some of them put forward the same effort, but somehow they weren't quite as successful. I was losing self-esteem. Certain people made fun of me, claiming I had a college education with no occupation, speaking rude calling me an intellectual fool. My vocabulary insulted their I.Q. as my way of retaliating for what they had to say.

My effort to retrieve my dignity was to write words to read in fiction novels, creating a life of a better existence, and I was having fun with my writing skill. I was over indulging in my drinking, serving less fortune women as their penis technician. After several years of living with my mother, things got worst; I even seek the advice of a Psychic, thinking that someone may have put a curse against me living the lifestyle of my desire.

I was motivated by this certain lady entering my dream, and she inspired me to enhance my abilities: mental, emotional, and physically, because I had the potential to succeed in activating the initiative of my mentality to fulfill the lifestyle of my desire, and a few days later, I was forced to relocate in the state of Texas. I had to live with a relative I didn't appreciate.

Five months later, I received an occupation; I finally got a job as a temporary worker at the post office. I was making two third less than their regular workers, doing the same type of labor. Although I had passed the post office test, I had to accept this type of salary, and I made enough money to move into an apartment of my own. I worked for the post office for six months, before I was laid off, and rehired for another six months. This type of situation was making me frustrated.

People in Texas were going to jail, and after they were released, they would get a job, paying more money than what I was receiving, and because of my economic existence, the ladies in those areas of dating were unappreciated. They seem to have some kind of drug problems. Rock cocaine was a drug epidemic making black women addicted to it, causing them to lose their dignities. They would do just about anything for a hit of that rock- up cocaine. They were known as crack heads, performing the cheapest form of prostitution known, fellatio, regular or anal intercourse, and some of these ladies once lived a life with middle class prestige. Now that they have lost everything, and if it took an additional two dollars to soothe their craving to suck on that glass pipe with a piece of rock cocaine inside it, they will become a two dollars hooker.

Each time I would lost interest in my effort of becoming successful, I will reiterate this dream about a beautiful woman motivating me to continue pursuing more diligently my attempt to prevail over whatever existing against my effort of becoming successful. I called her Miss Pulchritudinous. Most people who associated with me knew of her existence from the way I talked about meeting such a female human being.

I was hired by another federal government agency, Food and Drug Administration; there I was a temporary worker for two years, utilizing my skill for less pay. I was saving my money to buy me a car, but I resigned from the mail and file clerk position with F.D.A., because I felt that the Administrative Officer had me in an unfair position. Some black people in certain ranking positions as government officials are misusing their positions by taking the advantage of their own kind by hiring other blacks as cheap labors giving themselves a reputation.

I moved to the state of Washington in search for a better life. When I got there, I thought that I must be still under a curse, because my job situation there was just as worst. I became a temporary worker on Fort Lewis Army Post with a little prestige as a Military Personnel Clerk. A spouse was hired, and I permanent position was denied. My situation with jobs and ladies were unappreciated.

I can't remember a Valentine's Day, when I was with a lady I could appreciate. I wrote about moments of romance and how to enchant a lady's mind on this particular day when love is celebrated. It was the year of nineteen ninety-five on the night of February the fourteenth. Once again she invaded my dream with a more serious effort to motivate me to continue to be successful. I was once again unemployed without a job, one family member, and a couple of so-called friends were concern about the condition I was in. Here I am away from home, and things for me there were going wrong.

Once again the lady of my dream visited me, the most beautiful creature, God have created is a lady. I have never seen such a beautiful female human being, looking like an angel in flight, invading my dream again on this Valentine's night. She came flying through the ceiling of my bedroom; as though, she was a ghost, with clear water like image of her physical existence. I was wandering why this was happening to me, and if this was considered a nightmare, I didn't mind about seeing her there. Out of frustration, I did body developing exercises to look more rejuvenating for my age. As middle-weight man, I have somewhat of an attractive face. I stood at a height of five feet nine, physically, I considered myself fine, and every now and then, I would advertise the stimulating qualities of my masculinity, trying to bring out the femininity of each lady I meet, but this lady of my dream was a unique human being. Someone I will love to meet in reality, seeing her landing on my bedroom's floor, smooth and slow. She was captivating to see, I couldn't believe this was happening to me on February the fourteenth, Valentine's night while I was asleep. It seems like a movie of suspense staring me.

When she landed on the floor, her wings folded and vanished from her body, there she stood looking like a nude goddess. Then her body became more colorful as clothes appeared there making her fully dressed, judging by her physical characteristic, she seems to be borne of mixed nationalities, Italian-Porto Rican was her identity. Her glowing smooth pinkish tan complexion seems to be a blessing, from her head to her toes, the sight of her eyes pleasing quality showed. Her face was cuter than any flower known, perfectly developed in an oval shape, and she was looking at me in a teasing way.

Her pretty eyes were exquisite enough to hypnotize. They appeared to be clear, round, sexy and dreamy, bright bluish green in color with dark honey brown centers and trimmings to enhance her cute face's appearance. Her eyes were in the company of natural brows and lashes. The loveliness of her eyes seems to gleams out sparkles whenever she gave me a sexy smile, showing off the sparkles of her pretty white teeth, shining through her enchanting lips, appearing to be kissable sweet.

There was a small sexy black pimple of a mole, setting uniquely on her face's cheek at a distant from her nose and top lip. Everything seems to be prefect about her appearance. She looked good enough to eat. Her hair was naturally curly, dark in color, passed her shoulders in length, styled to enhance her cute face's appearance.

She stood at a height any man would like, five feet seven or maybe nine; she was one of a kind. She possessed the body's weight any lady would appreciate looking this great. Her body had an incredible shape. Her shoulders, arms, and hands would bring elegance to the eyes of any human being, and she had a body figure that met this description: thirty-six, twenty- four, and thirty-seven. She had the body of Miss Heaven, full at the chest with erection causing, mouthwatering breasts, each had a three dimensional figure with erected nipples. I have never seen a pair of tits looking so delicious. I would like to devour an osculating technique on each of them.

Her clothes would vanish off and reappear on her body, as she walked around my bedroom looking like a love goddess. She had a flat sexy stomach with a stimulatingly slim waist line and from behind, that part of her body, extended salaciously out and curving round into a piece of flesh, with the figure of a full round upside down heart of Valentine's, with deep curving cheeks, making her butt look seductively lovely, connecting to the thighs of the world most beautiful pair of legs, splendidly developed, long, healthy and sexy, slightly bow at the knees. She was borne to please, nice size feet with cute toes to play with.

The appearance of her nude body was causing me sexual problem, like an aphrodisiac, she was enhancing my appetite. The sight of her pretty legs had me craving, knowing that it will be like heaven, just to see such loveliness spread, and between her gorgeous thighs was that special part of her gender, that make a man feel like paradise. What a euphoric feeling? A woman like this can cause a man like me to witness?

This what makes a man becomes a womanizer, seeking the qualities of different women's vagina, but the vulva of this lady's crotch was a piece of puffed flesh covered with dark curly pubic. I began to think somewhat stupid. "Damn, she even has a pretty cochin." Her panties and bra reappeared on her body, then a thin sheered grown covered the rest of her, she walked around my bed as though she was modeling.

I began to witness her intellectual qualities, she possessed a high I.Q. with a good attitude, stimulating my mood, she's mentally clever while utilizing her articulated skill, convincing my mind while pleasing my ears, and her soft sweet voice brought pleasure to my heart. I was ambiguously delirious of what I was witnessing. This seems too real to be a dream. She also proved that she could dazzle me with her enchanting personality.

She slowly walked toward me, lying in bed, and politely sat beside me there. Her personal hygiene was nose pleasingly clean. She smelled fresh and sweet to me in this dream. She stared at me with the look of being sincere, as she serenaded my ears with words I loved to hear. "Bobby, I'm someone you should meet in reality, because I believe you are the husband I need, from the survey I did on you, proved that your masculinity, inspired me to invade your dream, on this Valentine's night, February the fourteenth, I'm here to indulge with you intimately. It will be a miracle, if this does happen to us in reality, together darling, we can produce a family of siblings, and rear them up to become intellectual individuals."

I was breathless while hearing this gorgeous looking lady advocates her interest in marrying me. This dream was alleviating all the frustrations, I was witnessing, before I sadly fell asleep, filled with animosity toward my total existence, with a feeling of callosity. Now I feel as mellow as a floating feather, what a euphoric feeling this dream had me witnessing? I was feeling so high and nice. There isn't a drug ever been invented, that can make me feel better than the thrill I was witnessing.

She continued enchanting me with words, describing the way our lives should be in reality, speaking convincingly. "Wouldn't it be nice, if you and I were spouses, living a lucrative lifestyle of our desire, while giving thanks to the living God of our lives, Jesus Christ for the blessing, he granted to us through love and trust. By the way, tonight is my birthday, I was borne on this day, February the fourteenth, and this is the reason why I'm here invading your dream. I'm somewhere in my twenties, young, intelligent and tender, yet I'm firm and mature enough to be your only lover."

She stopped talking, and gave me a wink of an eye with a sexy smile. I have always been emotionally vulnerable by the appearance of a beautiful woman. Now I'm intimidated, because she is looking at me in a flirtatious way. I began to fear, that the consequent of this dream, maybe detrimental to my emotional interest. She spoke as though she was hearing my thoughts. "No, please don't think negative about this situation, I'm here to motivate you, to enhance your existence rejuvenatingly. Enlighten your mentality, be clever enough to persuade the minds of others."

My conscience spoke again. "Remember, this is only a dream, she is one piece of good loving, you will never indulge." Then she spoke assuringly to me, "Bobby, think positive, control your conscience, this is your dream, and you can make love to me, if I may insist, it's the way I want it to be. But in reality, you will have to be perspicuous enough to achieve your own destiny. Strengthen your emotion courageously with a convincing amount of confident in your ability to achieve the lifestyle of your dream."

She hesitated while looking at me in an admiring way, and then I heard her say, "You look great for a man your age, and physically you are continually rejuvenating yourself, just as eyes pleasing as you can be. No matter how old you live to be, try to maintain that stimulating quality of your masculinity, and also try to perform with outstanding agility, because there is always room for improvement."

I looked into her beautiful eyes as I replied, "You are my inspiration." She gave me a surprising look with a smile on her face, and I heard she say, "You are my desire. My name is Brilisa in this dream. We may miss each other in reality, because there are certain jinx and curse, pending against us, but nothing can prevent us from indulging sexually in this dream."

Those words caused my manhood to come alive, as we stared into each other's eyes. She cuddled herself cozily against me. Our lips met with a gentle kiss, and we prolonged it passionately. Her tongue tasted naturally sweet, and I enchanted her with a French kiss. This began our foreplay technique. Her nightclothes vanished from her body once more, as she cuddled her nice warm body against mine.

I made oral love to her, as though she was something delicious to eat, devouring a nipping, licking and sucking technique, from her lips to her feet, licking in and around her ears, titillating the nipples of her breasts with my tongue and lips collaborating in awaking all of her sexual nerves. Her sexy moan encouraged me to move on.

I kissed on down between her highs, enjoying the taste of her paradise. I stay there, cunnilingusing her for a while. We indulged into the physical art of making love. I inserted into her warm, wet, stretching to fit vagina, performing the skill of a penis technician, causing Brilisa, my miss pulchritudinous to experience the joy of her life, multiple orgasms were erupting between her thighs, and spreading joyfully throughout her inside.

She began to moan, soft and sweet, these words into my ears. "Hummm, Bobby, baby, yes, I do adore your lovemaking skill. It feels so innovatingly great, the way you copulate, with vibrating movement of your body, filling my inside with so much pleasure, I can't baby, just can't control my moans, oh God, Bobby, you are making me feel so good inside, making love with you is so much fun. I'm about to come, experiencing another thrill of life, so intensify, I want to be your wife, because you make me culminate so great."

I began to enhance the movement of my body, and she began to moan into my ear seductively, as though she was hollering. Our bodies were wet with sweat. We began to kiss, and suck on each other's lips expressing ourselves. She moaned out loud. "Thank you, baby, for making me feel so sensational." I replied, "I want to express my gratitude, for making me feel this fucking good." It wasn't long, before I began to moan alone with her, as we culminated into the most breathtaking, eyes stretching, nose opening, fingers and toes spreading, thrills of life erupting twice. My ejaculation was so strong, flooding her vagina with my sperm.

I was still lying there, between her beautifully smooth legs, sexually enervated, when I heard her said. "Goodbye, my love, I hope to see you again in reality." Then she just vanished from lying beneath me. I awaken, from this dream wet with a lingering thrill, and a smile on my face, because it seemed so real. I was inspired by this dream to write poems, describing her existence with a picture of me talking about my personality with more poetry about her femininity, and a story of our relationship written fictionally.

(Sugar Terrific) Romance Wilson

This is the writing ability of me with such pseudonym describing my personality, possessing a soothingly smooth attitude, considerable and kind are the thoughts of my mind, collaborating with the courageous feeling of my heart, giving me such confident, because I believe in the existence of God. My faith will never depart. I'm also a person with mixed feeling about the life I am existing, if I am approached the wrong way, I'm not the type of person who is quick to retaliate, I believe in releasing and forgiving, because I know if I hold a grudge, then a grudge will be hold against me, keeping the blessing I need away from me.

I want to live the lifestyle of my desire. The way I described it to be praying to the Holy Trinity diligently, because I grew up observing and studying the existence of other people, analyzing their individualities: mental, emotional and physically, I find people in general as a group of interested human beings. I'm not that much of a talker, because to me people in general like to argue.

I'm more of a listener. I pay attention to what I need to hear, and I do express my opinion, because I'm concern about women individually. The most beautiful creature to me, God has ever created is a lady. Such a human being invaded my dream, motivating me to enhance my existence. I believe in the Holy Trinity, and that my ethnicity contributed to my appearance, and the authority of my writing skill with the right and power to reveal the way I feel, quoting words better than what I have heard.

Romance is the intellectual literature that I do. I believe that knowledge is the most powerful aspect of life, if an individual has the wisdom to utilize it right, in an understandable and convincing way. Using words like this is my way to play, entertaining readers is my ability, enhancing such characteristic is the existence of Bobby R. Wilson. Mental, emotional and physically, I'm trying to be the best that I can be. This is my prerogative, writing words to read is my expertise, hoping for the chance to receive such prestige, pertaining to this skill, I majored in as my education, hoping and praying that someday, I can profit from it as my occupation.

I have learned what is takes to be an intelligent human being with the use of common sense to be polite and kind with an admirable personality, intellectually speaking, I try to treat people the way I want to be treated equal and respectfully. I have a terrific attitude, and concern about everyone who was borne, because to me human beings in general are mysterious people. Each person has a unique characteristic, about his or herself, that makes them different individually from other people, take me for instant romance is my expertise, whether it's writing words to read or pleasing women intimate needs. I can exaggerate by writing what I have to say.

I put forward diligent effort to be successful, learning what it takes to be more appreciated, trying to stay in shape by doing calisthenics, taking vitamins, nutrient supplements and cream, to rejuvenate my appearance, but age seems to be defying my existence, just like any other male human being, I'm trying to be eyes pleasing to see, with an intellectual personality, because I like pretty women of different nationalities.

Some of them possess intellectual attitudes, polite and smooth, I never misjudge their femininities, because they can also be mean and rude, but thank God for their existences, because they bring so much pleasure to my masculinity, putting me in competition with other men, trying to win their interest.

My relationship with women has been clandestine individually. What I have to say is for her ears to hear only, because I have more fun when I'm with a woman alone. I compromise with her existence, because I want her to enjoy every moment she shares with me.

I enjoy the skill of writing, because to me it is exciting, writing a book or poems about the existence of human beings, fiction or none, I probably can write lyrics to a song. To me this is fun, creating people of fiction existences with different characteristics. A writer can be what he or she wants to be, by writing words to read, controlling the relationship of the characters he or she creates, and by having the knowledge of different occupations, help bring life to his or her creation, and getting their work published can also be frustrated.

This pen name help to enhance my existence, it motivated my determination, because I know, I have to perform with efficiency. Life hasn't been too good to me, because I was borne with dark skin in a society like this, a country that racial prejudice was once its creed, now diversity is changing such a belief into equality, implemented by black leaders and members of other ethnicities, influencing politicians with liberal interests, that this country will be greater, if racism was eliminated, giving a poor individual like me a chance to achieve the lifestyle of his or her dream.

Changing the thoughts of other people that I'm inferior, because I am a member of the minority. I thank God, my mother and father, that I was borne to live, learning how to read, write and reason with the knowledge of arithmetic, also witnessing the lives of other human beings is a knowledgeable experience, I have received. No matter what their ethnicities maybe, I judge a person by his or her individuality, that what make life so unique to me.

The thing I may see, hear or read is a part of learning from each existence, because life is for people to live, and it involves the suffering of hating and the loving of each other. Who knows a foe may become a friend or when life is going to end. Respect and understand the existence of other people is a lesson all human being need to comprehend. Now here are some poems, written about this special female human being, describing her femininity.

Femininity

This is the quality of her gender
That most women are borne
To be soft and tender

A physical difference
From masculinity
As she ripen into maturity

She changes: mentally, emotionally and physically
Once a month she has to bleed
Some people think it's a curse

God placed against Eve
Now women of this world
Have to suffer too

There is no cure
That's not true
This is a nature cycle

Every lady has to mature through
Men are advised to comprehend
The condition these women are in

Once a month they become mentally rude
Emotionally cruel and physically aggravated
Because life affects them this way

As an individual all women are different
Some are in control of their personalities
Under these conditions

While others suffer from mental deficiency
By letting their thoughts affect their feelings
Their attitudes change like the seasons

Physically they swell
With an unpleasant smell
If their hygiene is not as clean

Cramping pains about to drive some insane
Under these conditions certain women's
Moods can be polite and cool

Like a nice sunny spring day
They refuse to let such discomfort
Of their monthly get in their way

Other women are not in such control
Their monthly cycle make them unfriendly and bold
When things are not going right

Their temperaments can be as hot
As a dry summer's night
If they can't have their ways

They can be as cold
As a freezing winter's day
And they can start an argument

In a bold way
The femininity of Miss Pulchritudinous
Is what I appreciate

About her existence
She doesn't allow her monthly cycle
To interfere with her lifestyle

During her most unpleasant condition
She can still negotiate
In a compromising way

She is willing to listen
Before having something to say
She doesn't let her physical condition

Get in her way
Her hygiene is controllably clean
Because she is an educated lady

With knowledge of her situation
And she participates with confidence
In her relationship

Her Mind and Emotion

This is the way she thinks and feels
Mentally and emotionally
She's in control of her existence
This is the spiritual part
Of her ability

The way she actually thinks and feels
Can't be witnessed by the eyes and ears
Of any other human being
Unless she says or does something
From that result

Her thoughts collaborate
With her feelings
Before she makes a decision
She analyzes the whole situation
Before she has something to say

She's an intellectual kind
Analyzes with her mind
And emotionally she evaluates
In a clever way, she's convincing
In expressing her opinion

The function of her brain
Makes her mind an incredible thing
With the help of her heart
Doing a fascinating job
She's a blessing from God

She's kind and feminine
And she's careful when expressing
Her thoughtful feelings
She doesn't want to offend
Anyone without intention

Don't get me wrong
She's not always cool and calm
She's a human being
Who can also make a scene
To defend herself with intellectual help

By the use of her mind
She's logically inclined
With a courageous feeling
Filling her with confidence
To succeed in what she attempts

This mental feeling that she witnesses
Makes her a sexy lady
She knows how to cooperate
While on a date
For love's sake

Her Physical Appearance

This is the part of her existence
That can be seen
Flesh, bones and blood
Are what her body
Is made of

Her body is covered
By a thin layer of skin
Known as her complexion
Showing off a beautiful color
Making her looks lovelier

Her stature is the height
In which she stands
With a body's weight
That is appreciated by her shape
Some parts are thick

The others are thin
A shape like this
She has to win
A beauty contest
Because she looks the best

The feature of her face
Is as cute as
A bright sun-shining day
With a breeze of fresh air
Blowing seductively through her hair

Her shoulders, arms and hands
Bring elegance
To the eyes of any man
Because they are smooth and sleek
With a massaging technique

The rest of her body
Is advertising her feminine quality
It's not her size
That hypnotizes my eyes
It's her shape

That makes her look so great
A blessing to her gender
Looking soft and tender
With a body's figure
Seductive to see stimulatingly

Her Personality

When she reacts from the way
She thinks and feels
It is known as her personality
A reflection of her mood
Produced by her attitude

This is what she may do or say
Physically or verbally
During a particular situation
Revealing the way she thinks and feels
Is her personality

This is what people witness
About her existence
Although she may be a beautiful lady
She may have some ugly ways
When she's negotiating

It depends on the mood of her attitude
Whether she's cool and smooth
Being polite
By saying or doing things
This is right

This is a temporary state
Of her mentality
Affecting the way she thinks and feels
She's not always polite and smooth
She can also be rude and cruel

Here's a situation while on a date
With someone she appreciates
She participates in a conversation
Revealing the way she thinks and feels
Verbally and physically

To impress her date
That she is interested in being his lady
From the way she presents herself
To the way she dresses and smells
Are parts of her personality traits

Educated or not
All people's temperaments get hot
As human beings
We all reveal
The way we think and feel

Characteristic Development

It's not that she's
Eyes pleasing to see
It's the way
She enhances her existence
Mentally, emotionally and physically

She developed her character distinctively
From an infant to a child
She matured through
Her adolescent lifestyle
To become a lady of her desire

She was cute as a girl
And she wanted to be
An intellectual lady
She took interest in higher education
To enlighten her mentality

With the knowledge of how to succeed
By comprehending the words that she reads
And writing words to express her interest
And performing the method of arithmetic
So that she doesn't get cheated

Emotionally she's concerned about her feelings
She wanted to be strong enough
Not to get hurt
She learned how to adjust her feelings
According to the situation

That she participated
She wanted to be physically healthy
By doing calisthenics

Her body becomes sexually developed
Every feminine part of her body reveals
Itself with seductive quality

She became the envy of most women
Because she is mentally sharp
Emotionally strong and physically firm
With a body figure

Eyes pleasing to see
Because she enhances
Her characteristics
With the qualities
Of Miss Pulchritudinous

Her Individuality

As an individual
Her nationality can be different
From her ethnicity
Her nationality is the country
She was born in

And her ethnicity
Is her physical characteristics
Similar to other people
For instance, if her ethnicity is Caucasian
It doesn't mean that

She was born in the United States
Or if she's black
Doesn't mean she's from Africa
Or because her gender is feminine
Doesn't mean her sexuality

Attracts her to men
Unless she's heterosexual
Then men have her blessing
As an individual
She is different from other women

Even if she has a twin
She is different
By the way she thinks and feels
It's not her nationality
Or her ethnicity

That impresses me
It's her individuality
That I'm interested in
Her as a female human being
Mentally, emotionally and physically

It's all about her individuality
The way she looks, thinks and feels
Her religious characteristics
Can be identified
With other people

She shares the same belief
As some of them
But the way she appeals
Makes her different
As an individual

She is logically inclined
By the use of her mind
Her emotion
Is compassion with love
When her thoughts influence her feelings

She reacts willingly
This is her personality
She has the desire
To choose her own lifestyle
With a person of another gender

Living together as spouses
Husband and wife
Producing a family of siblings
Being sisters and brothers
To one another

Being a mother
As an individual
She is more loving

An inspiration to her husband
And an admiration to others

As an individual
Her physical characteristics
Meet such a description
Different parts of her body
Advertising different qualities

Cute Sensation

It is always enticing
For me to see
Her cute face's appearance
Captivating my emotional interest
Heartwarmingly

Dazzling my eyes
With her enchanting smile
As though I was hypnotized
By her lovely face
Oval is its shape

Smooth is the texture
Of her complexion
Her hair, eyes
Nose, lips, and chin
Collaborated in making

The appearance of her cute face
No matter what
The size, shape
Or color of her face
This is the part of her body

That will be seen every day
Acnes, pimples or just bad complexion
There are some faces
That need cosmetic blessing
Such as powder and cream

If she uses it right
Her face will become a beautiful sight
If there's a mole on it
Giving her sex appeal
Enhancing her eyes, nose and lip

Remember that beauty is only skin deep
And ugly is to the bone
No matter how homely
Her face may be
Cosmetics will enhance her appearance

The shape of her face
Pleases my eyes
In an influencing way
Featuring lovely eyes
Nice ears and a cute nose

With a pair of kissable lips
Convincing me to listen attentively
As her eyes and lips collaborate
With what she has to say
I must admit

There's not a doll ever invented
Nor a flower created
Or a car modeled
With a prettier shape
Than her captivating face

Beautiful Hair

Her hair passes her shoulders in length
It's styled to enhance
Her cute face's appearance
The style of her hair
Helps bring out the feature

Of what she wears
Some women wear their hair
In different colors and length
Long, kinky, straight
Curly, cut low or in a fro

Blonde, red, auburn
Brunette, brown or black
The color of their hair
Sort of expresses themselves
A head full of curls

Looks better on some girls
Styling it in a fro
These ladies seems to be on the go
Some hair is worn straight
To enhance the features of their faces

Ponytail with a bang
Shows the adolescent style
Of sexy fame
Hair has body Hair has style

There's a profession
Who knows how
To make hair look better
Ladies will always have to pay
To keep their hair looking great

Hair is worn long
For the feminine fun
Hair is worn short
For ladies who want to look stocky
Because it's their fault

Her hair is beautiful
No matter how she wears it
Just since it's neat
In its appearance
Like the hair of pulchritudinous

Feminine Eyes

Because of their colors, texture and size
Some ladies have beautiful eyes
Clear, round, sexy and dreamy
Females' eyes are sexy
Whenever you see them

Gleaming out a warm, sensational glimpse
That seems to sparkle
Whenever they wink
Their eyes seem lovelier
When they are of different colors

Light, dark or in between
Brown, blue, hazel or green
They can be slant
And still they are beautiful
To be seen

Those eyes with not a clear vision
Contact lenses not only
Help their situation
They also make
Their eyes look great

The eyes of Miss Pulchritudinous
Are worth seeing
Bright bluish green in color
With honey-brown centers and trimmings
They look sexier when she is grinning

Two lovely colors I adore seeing
Showing the characteristics
Of her gender
Soft and tender
My love for her I have to surrender

When she gives me
That sexy look
I can tell that she's
In an intimate mood
Her eyes seem to express her attitude

Females' eyes can be dressed
To look their best
Whether they are large or small
Their eyes show
The feeling of their hearts

Their eyes can help express
The words coming from their lips
Making a conversation
More convincing to hear
Pleasing the ears with sincere

Ladies' eyes are reluctant to lie
The truth shows the way they look
Happy or sad
To have eyes this beautiful
They should be glad

An eye for an eye
And a tooth for a tooth
Ladies' eyes improve
The way their faces look
In this book

Enchanting Lips

Her lips appeared
To be kissable sweet
With such enticing movement
When she speaks
Filling my eyes and ears

With the pleasant sight
And sound of her beautiful voice
Utilizing her articulated skill
With lips appeal
This is the part of her mouth

That catches attention
When her lips start
Moving people listen
Some women's lips
Are too thin to see

While others are
Too thick to miss
All lips can be used intimately
As a kissing technique
Soft and sweet

Lips this cute
I will love a wet kiss from you
It will put heat in my pants
Seducing my intimate mood
To get serious with you

I'm addicted to her cute lips
I crave to kiss them
Because their appearance
Is stimulating to see
With the fresh smell of her breath

Makes her kisses the best
We are osculating
When our lips caress
Against each other
And we are mouths loving one another

When our lips connect together
Prolonging a tongue-sucking hug
Awaking our sexual urge
Lips are used to speak
When we have something to say

They are also used to participate
In a foreplay technique
Her enchanting lips
Are delicious to kiss
With such a seductive touch

Urging me to go farther
Around her neck, into her ears
Kissing causes sex appeal
Lips like hers
Will make me fall in love

Back, Shoulders, Arms and Hands

These are the parts
Of her body hardly mentioned
But they also catch attention
Her back in an evening grown or a dress
Opens to show that aspect

Smooth and sleek
Her back is worth seeing
Glowing out its lovely color
While the rest of her body is covered
With clothes

Her back seduces me
Showing the quality of her femininity
Along with her elegance shoulders
As bare as they can be
Yet and still

They are eyes pleasing to see
Sleek is her shoulders' appearance
Showing off the feminine quality
Of her sexy body
Smooth and tender

I can't resist the thrill
I get each time
She wraps her lovely arms
Around me cuddlingly
Warming my emotions sincerely

With a cozy hug
The feel of her arms
Made me fall in love
I also enjoy holding
Her pretty, soft hands

A soothing feeling invades
My emotional interest
Each time she places
Her soft hand into mine
I become stimulated

As though it was foreplay technique
Every parts of her body I adore
Her arms give me such a cozy hug
With such a firm grip
Of her hands massaging me

With the softness of her fingertips
What a pair of hands
Elegant and neat
Romancing me sincerely
With her massaging technique

There are certain dresses
That she wears
Her shoulders are bare
And her back is being seen
She's always an elegant lady to me

Lovely Breasts

My compliment to the exquisite
Appearance of her chest
When she is wearing a low-cut dress
The cleavage of her breasts
Looks it best

Two full and erected pieces of flesh
Protruding with a shape
I as a man
Will deeply appreciate
Seeing such a dimensional figure

Looking like two lovely-sized peaches
With her nipples
Being the tip of each peach
They are seductive to see
Standing free

This is one
Of her physical aspects
Different from my gender
I'm talking about being feminine
Now there are some women

Who are neglected
When it comes to growing breasts
They are just as flat
As some men
By the chests

To receive full breasts
They need surgical help
Most women with little or no breasts
Most likely their panties
Are full of flesh

That looks their best
I'm talking about their butts
It's not the size
But the shape of her breasts
That makes them look their best

Such an appearance improves
When they are erected
Her full, firm breasts
Are the thrills of her chest
With an attempt to be caressed

A picture of such loveliness
Should always be seen
Her breasts fit her blouse or shirt
Full of lust
They are also lovely to touch

Stomach and Waist

This is the part
Of her abdomen
That makes her
A sexy-looking woman
Her waist and stomach

She has a flat, sexy stomach
With a slim waistline
Which makes her look so fine
She is a great-looking lady
And her stomach and waist

Help give her body such a sexy shape
With a cute navel
The slimness of her waist
Contributes to the sex appeal
Her butt and hips reveal

Extending out and round
Into a figure so fine
To see eyes pleasingly
Lovely enough
To be touched seductively

Her stomach is that part
Of her body
That swells when she gets pregnant
With a baby
Some women look better that way

A special gift
To her gender
I appreciate a lady
Who keeps her body in shape
Pregnant or not

It's her fault
If she eats a lot
And becomes overweight
Out of shape
And unappreciated

It's her job as a woman
To keep her body looking sharp
Because physically
She is more eyes pleasing to see
Than any other female human being to me

She can even warm the hearts
Of other female human beings
With masculine mentality
By her feminine appearance
Eyes pleasingly

Her sexy stomach and waist
Catch more attention on swim days
While she is on the beach
Wearing a pair of bikinis
Advertising the sexy quality

Of her feminine body
Women today are more conscious
Of their physical shapes
They know that a healthy body looks great
Especially their stomach and waist
Seductive Butt

As far as my eyes can see
She has a pretty booty
My compliment to her behind
The sight of it
Is magnificently fine

A piece of flesh well developed
This part of her body was blessed
With a figure better
Than a love goddess Her butt is gorgeous

Starting from the slimness
Of her waistline
Extending outward and round
Forming a unique figure
Curving seductively at each cheek

Connecting to her beautiful thighs
Eyes pleasingly
I have to look at it twice
Her behind is built so fine
Just as nice

As an upside-down
Heart of valentine
From the front
She is a feminine hunk
And from behind

Her butt captivates the mind
Of any human being
Seeing it in a pair of jeans
The figure of it
Is very unique to see

It is also seen in a dress
Putting her gorgeous legs
Into competition
Trying to look the best
There are some women

Who don't wear a bra
Because they don't have enough breasts
To advertise their chests
But their panties are full
Of good-looking fleshes

It doesn't matter
About the size
It's the shape of her booty
That makes it looks so great
There are different features

To see from a female's front
But a man will always smile
At the sight of a pretty rump
Some ladies' butts
Are as lovely as their faces

Especially if they possess
That heart of Valentine's shape
Her pretty booty
Will always be appreciated
In a stimulating way
Splendid Development

From her pelvis
To her sexy feet
There are two
Lengths of fleshes
I love to see

Long and healthy
Smooth and sleek
They move her body physically
Heaven will be my blessing
To see such loveliness spread

I'm talking about
Her sexy-looking legs
When she is wearing a dress
They look their best
In short pants or a swimsuit

The delightful appearance of her legs
Brings joy to my manhood
Because they look stimulatingly good
And the movement they make
Causes her butt to shake

Some ladies' legs come together at the knees
Others are straight or bow
Ladies with pretty legs like hers
Should always let them show
Themselves in a sexy way

During a beauty contest
Legs are there
To look their best
There are some luxurious legs
Ready to go to bed

Enticing to Me

This is the part of her body
That shows the true meaning
Of her gender

Feminine and tender
It's the good
Of her womanhood

Made to please my intimate need
The sight of it
Meets this description

Mounted fat and fine
Covered with pubic hair
Showing itself seductively

Between the thighs
Of her smooth, pretty legs
It's so plump

The crotch of her panties
Is stuffed with it like her rump
The figure of a woman's vulva

Is hardly mentioned
When talking about her sexual appearance
It does have a description

This is the main part
That makes a woman different
From the other gender

If the orifice of her vulva
Is covered by a layer of skin
Known as a hymen

She is a virgin
Until it is broken in
Through the motion

Of sexual intercourse
When this happen
Her vagina will show

An elastic passage of flesh
That gets warm and wet
Ready for sex

When having sex it can
Contract and relax
To accommodate the insertion of a penis

And it can stretch enough
To give birth
To another human being

As an individual
Each lady is different
By the characteristic of her vagina

It has a figure
That is stimulating to see
With a temperature

To make a man feel good
There are some women
Who are sexually numb

To most men
They are no fun
Because they are frigid

And most likely they prefer
To have sex with other women
But those who are nice, warm and wet

With a pleasant fit
Will always keep men interested
In their intimate needs

This is the glory
Of their womanhood
Whether it looks bad or good

And without a doubt
This is what makes a man
Choose a woman to be his wife

Maturity

A stage of development
A person goes through
Mentally, emotionally and physically

From the day of birth
To the day of decease
Like a fruit on a tree

That blooms into existence
From a flower of that tree
It starts off small and bitter

Green and unripe to eat
As time prolongs
It grows big and strong

Changes color
And its form
Sweet and ready to be eaten

Because it has reached maturity
The ripe stage of its existence
If it hangs around too long

It will rot
Overripe due to longevity
And fall from the tree

And deteriorate its existence
The life of a human being
Goes through a process like this

From birth a person
At least needs
The nursing of his or her mother

To prolong his or her existence
Until his or her senses
Develop enough to comprehend

The life of living
A human being ripened
Mentally, emotionally and physically

As he or she gets older
The way they think and feel
Are their souls

From an infant child
Of a young age
Learning how to walk and talk

Read and write
While growing into
Their adolescent stages

Better known as teenagers
Too old to be a child
And too young to be grown

They are considered
To be juveniles
These are the years maturity begins

In a human being
Mentally, emotionally and physically
Each gender begins

To show its difference
Mentally enhancing the wisdom
Of intelligence

Emotionally witnessing a feeling
Of strength and concern
And physically showing the quality

Of his or her body's figure
Being masculine or feminine
Each is a gender

At the age of twenty-one
He or she is
Considered to be grown

Mentally he or she has the ability
To teach what each has learned
The wisdom to carry on

Emotionally each has become
Stronger with confidence
To accept the hardship

Of life's existence
An experience of misery
Or a pleasure to remember

Physically he and she are capable
Of producing another human being
By indulging intimately

Just like the fruits
On the trees
He or she must decease

After a life of maturity
Longevity has to end
From green through ripe to rot

That's when the life
Of maturity stops
Ending the existence of living

Death is the beginning
Of something different
No one knows about it while living

A Woman, a Lover and a Friend

She is all three
As one human being
As a woman

Her femininity
Soothes me
Eyes pleasingly

She is physically equipped
With the best quality
Her gender
Has to present
She is fine
In body and mind

She is so calm
When I'm holding
Her in my arms

When we first met
She assured me
We will always be friends

She listens attentively
When I speak
And she always

Has something to say
To make my frustration
Go away

Comforting me with words
Of encouragement
And whenever I did

Say something
That she disagreed
We debated the issue

In a compromising way
This is how we negotiate
By listening to what

Each other has to say
And we would present
Ourselves to each other

In a stimulating way
She showed me more love
Than my own mother

Her concern was
Accurate and firm
This is a good woman

She didn't appreciate
Other people aggravating me
And when we indulged

Into the intimacy of making love
She made sure
That we made each other feel good

I have witnessed a feeling
Good enough to see
The result of it

And I was obligated
To make her feel
Just as great

As though we
We're producing a baby
We vowed to always

Be there for each other
Doing more to impress
One another

As time passed onward
Our love got stronger
Eventually she became

The mother of my child
The woman of my life
I asked her to be my wife

As a woman she's wonderful
As a lover she comforts me like no other
As a friend she's there assisting me through thick and thin

As a wife she makes life with me so nice
And as the mother of my child
She makes parenthood feel so good

She even participates in activity
Of the community
Impressing other people

As though she's
A politician selected by them
As her constituency

She is well represented
Doing things to improve the community
While producing a family of siblings

With me
Our lifestyle is exactly
The way I desired it to be

This how I met such a lady as she, I was an unpublished writer, suffering as a victim of plagiarism. I knew something has to be wrong with my expertise writing words to read, and I did it with ease and convincingly. I have a degree in that professional field, but each time I submitted some of my writings to a literary agency, publishing companies or other places of businesses getting rich off of unknown writers skills. Then from two or more months later I would receive the original copies of my writings with a letter expressing their regret of not being able to have my book published at this time, but somewhere in the future my style of writing will be marketable.

I was so disgusted with my failing effort, trying to be successful in the field of my profession, until one day I was discussing my situation with a coworker, and he suggested in a joking way that I should contact a lawyer, because he believe that my writing a lot of businesses have gotten rich by plagiarizing other people work.

He told me about this female attorney, young and very attractive in her appearance. I thought he was exaggerating about her looks, and he warned me that she was expensive, because she is a winner of all the cases she accepted as a challenge. She had won a lawsuit case for him, and he would talk to her about the possibility of having my writing stolen from me.

A few days later, I received a phone call from my coworker; Sal and he gave me the name and telephone numbers of this female attorney. I gave her a call to set up an appointment to discuss my situation with her, and she told me to bring some of my writings, the names, address, and telephone numbers of the different places of businesses where I submitted my writing.

The day of my appointment with her, I arrived early at the modern sky scrapper building in the middle of down town Portland City. Her office was located on the seventh floor of this building where most people go for legal assistant. At the door of her office the name of her and her profession was written Ms. Ulrica V. D'Angelo attorney at law.

When I entered her office, her secretary or paralegal, an attractive female human being greeted me, but not nearly as eyes pleasing to see as the person I came to see. Sarah was the name of Ms. D'Angelo paralegal. I told her that I have an appointment with Ms. D'Angelo, after that Sarah gave Ms. D'Angelo's office a buzz on her telephone. A few moments later, a fine sexy looking lady, expensively dressed in a short shirt suit came walking toward me where I was sitting in the lobby of her office.

The sight of her beautiful legs caught my attention eyes pleasingly as she walked closer toward me. My mouth agape with the stare of my eyes as they began to travel from the sight of her pretty lets upward, marveling the salacious figure of her body, and from the way her coat was fastened across her chest, I knew she had beautiful breasts. I heard her speaking to me. "Hello, Mister Wilson, I'm Ulrica D'Angelo attorney at law."

The sound of her polite and influencing voice enchanted my heart, as my eyes met hers. I stood up as she extended her hand to shake mine. She had a smooth firm grip, and I was astounded by her attractive face's appearance. She was a dark-complexioned Caucasian lady with a pair of colorful eyes; attractively bluish-green in color with honey brown centering and trimming of make them look lovelier.

This lady has a unique face's appearance with naturally long dark eye lashes and brows, a cute nose and a pair of soft kissable looking lips as she smiled greeting me, her eyes seems to gleams with the sparkles of her pretty white teeth, and there sitting at a unique distant from her nose and top lip, on her right face's cheek was a black pimple of a small mole adding sex to her cute face appearance.

Her hair passed her shoulders in length, black in color, naturally curly, styled to enhance the appearance of her cute face, and she led me into her office. I got a look at the figure of her behind, man! God must have blessed this lady with such a gorgeous body. Her butt possessed salacious quality.

Inside her office, the furniture showed her expensive taste. She invited me to a seat, and she examined my writing samples and the places of businesses, I had sent my writings to. Ms. D'Angelo read some of my writings, and was impressed by the content of my manuscript. The words of my poems caused her to give me a firm smile before she replied. "Mr. Wilson, from what I have read, you possess great writing skill, and there's possibilities that people have been stealing your writings or the ideas from it, but you can see by the way I'm dressed, and the appearance of my office, I'm an expensive lawyer. Are you sure? You can afford my service."

I gave her my award-winning look for sympathy as I replied, "Ms. D'Angelo, I was hoping that we could compromise on a proposition of you receiving 50 percent of the proceeds or the profit recovered from those who have stolen writing from me. You know the history of most new writers; most of us are living a life of poverty. I'll be mush oblige if you will show there's kindness in your heart to help me, and if there's any way I can return such a favor. I'm there at your request."

Ms. D'Angelo gave me a heart-warming smile as she replied, "I bet you have charmed the hearts of different ladies with your sad sensation conversation. I'll tell you what I'm going to do. I'm look into this plagiaristic situation for you at my convenient, since you have no money to invest up front, and I'm to keep all of the material you brought with you for collateral, give me a week or two, and I want 10 percent more than what you offered me."

I replied, "Okay, you got the best of me." She stood up from sitting behind her desk, and walked toward me. We shook hands to seal our deal. She then walked me out of her office replying, "Good luck, Mr. Wilson, you will be hearing from me."

It was about three and a half week later, when I received a telephone call from this attorney lady, and from the sound of her voice I was optimistically anticipating on hearing something good, she had to tell me. She replied, "Hello, Mr. Wilson, how are you doing today, this is your lawyer Ulrica D'Angelo. I have some good news for you. Matter of fact, I will like to invite you out for dinner at my expense. How long will it take you to prepare yourself for this occasion? Dress to impress, because I'm coming to pick you up at your address."

I was amazed to hear the voice of this beautiful lawyer inviting me out for dinner. My heart increased its beats as I began to breathe heavily, trying to compose myself as I replied. "Give me about an hour to shower and shave, and to find my best suit to wear for this special occasion." She replied, "Do you like seafood, lobster or shrimps, maybe a steak mixed in such a delicious taste?" I replied, "Yes, I can enjoy eating any kind of food with you, sound like this dinner invitation is a form of celebration."

Ms. D'Angelo replied happily, "Yes, it is, I caught up with the theft of your manuscript, and I had to go out of state, and legally fight them on their own ground. I also involved the F.B.I. to make them surrender the evident with a monetary apology. It was a book publishing company, making a lot of money from what you have written. They made a copy of your original manuscript. It's a good thing you gave me the copyright certificate to your book. I will tell you more about it, when we are eating, goodbye for now, Mr. Wilson, I'll see you when I come to pick you up for dinner."

After I hung up the telephone, I walked into my bathroom with a happy smile on my face, while taking care of my hygiene, showing, shaving and brushing my teeth, making sure my body was freshly clean and smelling good. I dressed myself in my best designer double-breasted suit, and it was fitting my body with eyes pleasing salacious quality.

An hour passed before I knew it, I heard my door's bell ring. I answered my door, and Ms. D'Angelo was standing there with a cute smile on her face. Her beautiful eyes were gleaming with the bright sparkles of her pretty white teeth. She was smelling expensively sweet with an elegant dress on, fitting her body with advertising quality. The cleavage of her breasts had stuff that part of her dress, as my eyes moved on down, the figure of her body looked renowned, slim waists, flat sexy stomach, a full round gorgeous-looking behind, even in that dress, the figure of her butt looked its best, and those long healthy and sexy looking legs of hers were a blessing to see. It would be a night of heaven to any man, she invites to her bed.

Ms. D'Angelo replied before I could speak. "Hello, Mr. Wilson, my-my- my what a handsome-looking client, I have here, my compliment to your appearance, more intelligent than I thought you would be." I replied, "Thank you, my lawyer, for such a flattering compliment, and you yourself look like a piece of human jewel, just as precious as you want to be. Would you like to come inside for a cup of coffee or a glass of tea?" She replied, "No thanks, maybe some other night, I'm here to take you out for dinner, and send some money on you, while discussing the possibility of our partnership."

We walked from my apartment to her car parked in the parking lot. A brand-new Lexus with an open in its roof so that we can see the moon during our night drive. The body of this expensive car was almost as fine as Ms. D'Angelo's body. This car was looking good, customized to fit Ms. D'Angelo's personality, intellectually attractive with sex appeal.

I assisted Ms. D'Angelo into her car by opening the door to the driver's side, and she politely seated herself behind the steering wheel. I gently closed the door, and as I began to walk toward the passenger's side, Ms. D'Angelo unlocked that side of the door for me. I heard the voice of a neighbor saying, "You all look at Bobby, that dude have luck up and find himself a rich good looking lady, Miss Pulchritudinous finally became a reality for him."

As Ms. D'Angelo drove away from that apartment complex, she replied, "I have recovered enough money from your stolen property for you to buy yourself a new car, a house or a more expensive apartment. You can also quit that physical laboring job, that you are so uncomfortable with, trying to get your foot into the door of your professional field, because I have a money making proposition, that you will love to hear."

After we arrived at this expensive restaurant, that I only heard people talking about the quality of it. I could hardly believe I was escorting this lovely looking Italian mixed with Puerto Rican lady into this place of elegance. I'm being the gentleman from my writing experience. When we got to our table, I gently pulled out a chair for her to sit.

After I sat at the table, we ordered a drink of French cognac to sip on while we decided what we would eat for dinner. Ms. D'Angelo ordered the same meal for me that she ordered for herself. As we ate our lobster, shrimp and steak dinner, she told me how she caught up with the publishing company that had profited over three million dollars from rewriting my manuscript titled: "The Enchanting Lover." My version of this character was black. This publishing company made him white to make more money.

There was also a contract signed by this publishing company with a motion picture industry to produce a movie from the story of "The Enchanting Lover." Ms. D'Angelo intervened on such a conniving scheme with a legal suit. Now the movie industry is negotiating with her as my legal adviser to compromise a deal. Although Ms. D'Angelo will receive 60 percent of the money I'm to receive from being of victim of plagiarism. She propositioned me to be the coauthor of this book, she wanted to write titled: "Miss Executive."

She got the idea to write such a book after she read a book of poems written by me titled: "Miss Pulchritudinous" She complimented my wisdom of women as an intelligent man seeking a woman who possesses high quality of prestige, and my writings have motivated her to advance in her professional interest. I agreed to be her coauthor, and she had written up a contract, legalizing us as partners with my signature to make it official.

This sounded like a money-making deal to me, here this attractive lady is offering me an opportunity to get rich, and before I met her, I wasn't making a penny from what I had written. Seemed like everybody and their mama envied my effort to be successful, until she took interest in representing me legally.

On different occasion, we talked about our social life, the different activities we participated in. We did have a few things in common. We like being in physical shape, and she requested that we should work out together. She even invited me to her house to do exercises with her. She has a room with different kinds of body developing equipments inside of it, and we could discuss business while working out together, challenging each other to do a certain amount of repetitions.

This dark-complexioned Caucasian lady had a body figure to please, talking about being a brick house or a bad mama jammer, foxy lady or any other words used to describe her stimulating appearance. She was Miss Pulchritudinous to me. From her head to her toes nothing but pure gorgeous of her body showed, and she worked out in spandex clothing. The figure of her butt and crotch were stimulatingly teasing me in her spandex bikini suit, from the back and front her outfit was stuff with eyes pleasing flesh, full of booty and vulva.

We were working up a sweat and Ms. D'Angelo's perspiration mixed with her perfume created a sensational scent that was really stimulating my olfactory nerve intimately, like it wasn't enough to seduce me with her appearance, and she had to add lust to my nose too. From the appearance of her bikini's bra stuffed with voluptuous breasts, she seems to be a perfect "C" cup. This lady is living a glamorous life. She also had a Jacuzzi in her house just before you walk out the door to her swimming pool. We worked out until all of her muscles were bluffly tight, then she invited me to sit in the Jacuzzi with her.

While sitting in the Jacuzzi together relaxing in this pool of heated bubbling water, Ms. D'Angelo told me that she also found a record company illegally using my poems for lyrics to different songs. I replied, "Wow, you are really getting rich off of me." She replied, "At least you are profiting from your expertise of writing words to read. I don't know why, but when I talk, you listen, and when you reply to what I have said, it is convincing to hear."

I replied, "Thanks, that sound like a compliment." Then she replied, "I'm thinking about working as an Assistant District Attorney. How would you elaborate your comments on what I just said?" I replied, "If you are as serious as you are beautiful, I think you will be very successful, speaking to convince the minds of those who hear your ears pleasingly hear warming voice, in other words you are persuasive enough to have a lot of criminals locked up."

Just as we began to admire each other's body while sitting in the Jacuzzi discussing her future interest, she received a telephone call, and she asked me to excuse her as she stood up and walked out of the Jacuzzi, and from the look of her butt, Ms. D'Angelo had some Negro's blood in her. That thin piece of material between her butt's cheeks caused me to witness an erection from the sight of her butt movement as she walked toward the telephone.

To my disappointment it was a call from a client, and we had to end our soothing warm wet discussion, so I got ready to go home, and she prepared herself to go and represent her client in trouble. She had some professional money making clients too, pro football, basketball and baseball players, also doctors and a few other elite people hiring her to defend their guilt's.

It was about a month, since I last saw Ms. D'Angelo, she would call me on the telephone to discuss the book we were writing together, and once again she invited me out for dinner to discuss future business as we sat enjoying our meal together. I replied, "Ms. D'Angelo," and she quickly interrupted me replying, "Bobby, please call me Ulrica, if you don't mind, I will like to be on a first name base with you."

I replied, "Okay, Ulrica, since you made us a lot of money, doing your job with honor, and as the coauthor of your book, if I do more than half of the work, I want to profit that much more than you, for instance, if I write 60 percent of the book, I want to receive 60 percent of its proceed."

Ulrica gave me an intimate smile as she replied, "Now I know why Miss Pulchritudinous invaded your dream, because she knew you two could motivate each other." I replied, "Yes, and what so delightful about that dream and reality is that you possess as far as I can see all the beautiful characteristics of Miss Pulchritudinous. To me you are an intellectually attractive female human being, an angel borne into this world with flesh, bones and blood."

Ulrica replied, "Thank you, sir, and I promise to represent her consummately. I will start next week working as an Assistant District Attorney. I want the challenge to see if I can convict criminals as well as I was defending them, and 1 think the justice system of this country is so what bias toward minority people."

I knew from her conversation that she would be doing some off the job investigation on her own, and she would be taking me alone with her for personal luck, so I decided to get a permit to carry a conceal weapon, and I suggested that she also obtain a permit to carry a gun of her own.

I decided to move into a condominium, and Ulrica assisted me in finding a nice expensive place to stay, because some of my female neighbors were trying to give Ulrica the wrong impression about our friendship. Just like a bitch literally speaking with a female dog's personality, trying to flirt with me whenever they see me in the company of Ulrica. Those same women had turned my approach down in the past, because I was poor and broke, trying to flirt with them, and they would quickly say, "Bobby, you know you don't have any money to be spending on a woman. I can't be nothing but your friend, because you don't make enough money to spend."

Now they are shouting out, "Hi, Bobby baby, when are you going to invite me out for a date. I have been saving it for you. It's warm, wet, ready and waiting." Ulrica would only smile with her reply. "When a man got money, he has no problem getting a woman." Ulrica went with me to buy a new car. We went to a Mitsubishi dealer, and I ordered a new customized Mitsubishi 300GT with a moon/sun roof, luxury interior with expensive wheels.

Then she showed me what she thought would be a nice place for me to live. It was an area of the city with nice-looking condominiums where affluent single people lived. Ulrica assisted me in buying new furniture for my new resident. She has good taste in interior design. I also had a room turned into a gym to do my calisthenics in, plus there was a Jacuzzi for a warm soothing relax bath.

Ulrica would come over and work out with me, once or twice a week, and sometime we would go jogging together in the park, especially uphill to release the stressful pressure of being a human being. We also went on several dates together. She wanted to mingle with the common or so called street people, observing their livelihoods. We even visited different types of nightclubs: Jazz, R&B, Pop, Rock also Country and Western clubs. We would have a drink or two, listen to the music, and observe the activities going on inside these places of businesses, while conversing or dancing together.

Ulrica was acting like a politician going to different places of businesses gaining recognition with each group of social people, and each type of nightclub we visited, we dressed ourselves according the environment we would visit. I would drive Ulrica to these different places, after a drink or two, she would socialize a bit with some of the people in the clubs, and we would dance until we were completely sober, then I would drive her home, and walk her to her front door while discussing what we were going to do the next night. At her door, she would walk up to me, and caress her body against mine with hugging arms while giving me a taste of her tender, sweet, kissing lips.

I never received such an erection so fast in my life. Each time 1 took her home after a date, she would say before entering her house. "Goodnight, Bobby, you were nice tonight, one of these nights while on a date with you, I'm be ovulating, and I'm seduce you in a intimate way, seriously I do appreciate your patient. I'm more interest in be successful with my effort of winning constituency than indulging sexually, but when it comes to being that type of woman, most likely you will be that man enjoying all of me, so good night and sleep tight, and if it bother you, take a cold shower."

While working as an Assistant D.A., Ulrica had added a goldish brown color to the front corner of her hair. It made her face looked lovelier, but her attitude was cruel, every case she prosecuted, she was determined to prove that the person was guilty of the crime he or she was accused of committing, and convicted him or her with jail time and a heavy fine.

The cases Ulrica prosecuted concerning domestic violent were attention catching, I went to court one day, just to see her perform her job, and she was dressed to impress in an expensively elegant dress, walking about the jury section, expressing herself to get a guilty verdict, and she would get a conviction at each case she prosecuted. If a man assaults a woman, she made sure he get jail time and a heavy fine. She also convicted a woman for scalding her husband with boiling hot acid water, disfigured her husband's face, because she caught him in the bed with another lady. This lady was charged with murder attempt, and she was sentenced to prison for five years.

Ulrica rented an old used car, and she asked me to stake out with her around different areas of the ghetto, and she wore old faded clothes. Those jean pants that she wore showed the figure of her behind like an upside-down heart of Valentine's, damn! She knew that she was physically fine. She was seeking to burst a police officer involved in crack coccocainee. He was on the take. The dealer was paying him to look the other way, and she succeeds in her task with a night vision video camera. She also prosecuted another high- ranking police officer for pimping prostitutes, forcing women to accost their bodies for him to profit.

Ulrica got upset with the justice department, when the D.A. refused to prosecute certain people for the crimes they committed, because of their status in the community. The prestige they had received, establish them with such reputations, the judge dismiss their cases. Since Ulrica had become well known to different fund raising organizations, and the women's club adored her, so she decided to run for District Attorney against her boss Jack Gordon, and with the help of the women's club, my strategy as her campaign manager, utilizing different aspect to convince the voters that no person is above the law, no matter what position he or she may be in or the amount of money they have. This strategy increased Ulrica popularity among her constituency, causing her to win the job of District Attorney.

There were speeches to attend, former dinner meetings, dances and banquets. I was meeting some of her former boyfriends and guys who had dated her in college and high school. Each of them tried to start another relationship with her. One or two of them were Caucasians men with ethnocentric attitudes, making remarks about she being in the company of an African-American man. "Who's he, your body guard or chauffeur dressed in a tuxedo?" She replied impudently, "No, this is Mr. Bobby Wilson, my emotional coordinator escorting me as my date. He is also my comfort, when I get lonely. We have a mutual relationship going on in which you really don't want to hear about it, since you got so near, but didn't succeed." This guy got upset, and he soon left the party with a frustrating look on his face.

New Year Eve night about two hours before mid-night, Ulrica and I arrived together at a New Year celebration, some of her clients, friends and associates honoring her for being the first female D.A. in the state of Oregon, talking about nominating her for the state Attorney General. This party was given on the top floor of a sky scrapping building located in the down town section of Portland, Oregon. There were people there representing each ethnicity showing pride in their nationalities.

The elevator ride had me sort of drizzle, escorting Ulrica, who was dressed in an elegantly body fitting blackish brown evening grown, with a split in the front and the back of her grown revealing the smooth flesh of her sexy back as well as her long, pretty, sexy legs, showing off themselves with each step she made, giving the guests eyes full of pleasure and the front of her dress was cut low enough to make her delicious appealing cleavage show. The people at this party were political friends, professional athletes, doctors, lawyers, a few movie stars, people working for the medias, business people and leaders of different communities there to celebrate the new year with the new D.A., and I was proud to be her escort, because being in the company of an intellectually beautiful woman to me was an honor.

I was dressed in a black tuxedo suit, looking good too; most of the men there gave me a wandering stare, when Ulrica introduced me to them as her date. I didn't know whether they were surprised to see her with a man of my ethnicity, escorting the lady more than a few of them once dated. I know the thought entered their minds whether or not we have encountered an intimate relationship, and I also knew from most of their faces impressions, most of them have tried, but weren't successful.

This party was on the fifty-seventh floors the rooftop of this building was covered by a glass dome. Ulrica was telling the different people greeting us that I was also the coauthor, utilizing the pen names of Thick Chocolate that's me and Creamy Caramel was her pen name, and some of the people at this party began to show more interest in me as a writer, and most of the women were interested in the way I philosophize the existence of life, and how I create fictitious characters existing in a scene so real.

I had to explain to those who were curious about how I excogitate with such vivid imagination, describing with words what my mind reveals to my eyes and ears. I also had to explain to them, writing nonfiction was more complicated than fiction, and my poems were written from a thought of a person, place or thing that have crossed my mind enough to influence my feeling, and the result of this action a poem is written. I try to use words that rhymes inform and entertain the readers.

I was impressed to see different type of people mainly women interested in my writing skill. One lady and I had engaged in a conversation about a story I had written, and I began to humor her with my way of describing certain scene, when other women began to gather around us and intervene our conversation with their questions of interest just to get my attention. Then the dialogue between them and me caused them to giggle, the fact of me being in the company of these women was flattering to me as a man catching their interests, so as I continued expressing myself, utilizing face and body gestures, mainly my eyes collaborating with the words coming from my mouth with a southern accent help them to visualize what I was saying.

Although Ulrica had most of the men attention, but on different occasions she excused herself from talking to them, and came over to interrupt my conversation with these ladies replying, "Will you ladies please excuse my intrusion, I'm sorry, but I have something to discuss with my escort lover, no, I mean coauthor, and it's urgent." Ulrica led me away from my admiring female audience with a jealous look on her face, as we arrived at the bar, she ordered two glasses of our favorite cognac replying to me, "Oh, I see that you can be very impressive in the company of women of different nationalities." I responded to her words this way. "If I didn't know better, Ms. District Attorney, I would say, you are a jealous lady."

Ulrica quickly replied, "Yes, you have intelligent knowledge about me, but there are some men in here who envy you catching the attention of most of these women. Miss Executive was well written and it is selling plenty, and the majority of these women here have a copy of it." I spoke in a curious voice. "What is written in that book, inspiring you to advance in your career?" Ulrica replied with bright shining eyes, "Yes, in many ways I'm still motivated by you, thanks, Bobby, baby, you are great." She gently kissed me on the lips, before turning to face the people of this party watching us, and gave them a wink of her eye with a smile replying, "Isn't he terrific?"

The band of this party started playing their music, and Ulrica requested a dance with me. We danced together for awhile, then one of her ex-boyfriend asked to cut in, before I could leave the dance floor, I was approached by a lady who wanted to dance with me, I dance with her for awhile, then her friend asked to cut it, and I ended up dancing with several women before the party was call to a stop to honor Ulrica as the unprecedented first female D.A. of that state.

Ulrica gave her acceptance speech, and expressed her gratitude toward my writing ability which motivated her interest to take such a challenge as this, and she admitted she doesn't know whether she will accept the challenge for Attorney General next on her agenda, but right now she's focusing on being the best D.A. this state had ever witnessed. She ended her speech at twelve o'clock mid night, and all the fireworks went off lighting up the dark starry looking sky with so many beautiful colors from the explosion in the air. All of this was visible through this glass dome covering the roof of this fifty-seven stories building. The people at this party were greeting each other with hands shake, hug and kisses, reciting the words. "Happy New Year!"

I was greeted by the men with a handshake, and words happy new year and congratulating me on the progress I was making with this intellectually attractive D.A. lady. Those men who had once gotten acquainted with Ulrica spoke low to me after their greeting. "Although she is a beautiful and intelligent lady, she can turn into a wild cat, and the result of such a selfish mean attitude can be detrimental to your emotional existence." I replied, "Thanks for the info, I will give that piece of advice some consideration."

As I was receiving hugs and kisses from most of the women at this party, I was observing Ulrica being greeted with hugs and kisses by the men at this party. I could tell the men, she didn't appreciate, because she would turn her face, so that they would kiss her cheek, instead of her lips, and she gave me a few unappreciative stare while a few ladies prolonged their lips against mine during their Happy New Year greeting.

The same chauffeur who drove the limousine with us to the party was the one driving us home. Ulrica gave him a big tip for missing this New Year celebration with his family members and friends. As we sit in the passengers section of this limousine on our way to Ulrica's house first. She and I had a bottle of champagne chilling on ice in the limousine's bar. We drank a glass of champagne, and Ulrica slid closer to me, and she let up the tinted window, so that the driver couldn't see us.

She began to express her appreciation for meeting me again, and before I could reply. Her soft sweet tasting lips were pressing against mine with a prolonged tongue inserting passionate kiss, and as she retrieved her tongue from my mouth. I invaded her mouth with my tongue, and things started to get sexually heated up in the back of that limousine.

We practically undressed each other, wow, this woman had the most beautiful erected and delicious-tasting breasts I have ever encountered in the history of my existence, and I was osculating such a sucking technique on each of her fully erected nipple as though I was a destitute baby hungry for his mother to breast feed him. While I was devouring a sucking technique on her breasts, I begin to caress my hand up her beautifully smooth legs, and she began to slowly spread them, inviting me to continue move on upward with massaging motion against her thighs, until I got to that lump of flesh, covered with hair, stuffing the crotch of her panties, as fat and as fine as it could be, looking like a bee hive between her thighs.

The crotch of Ulrica's panties became wet from my massaging technique, and I lifted the crotch of her panties up and pull it to the side, and inserted two of my fingers into her tight warm wet and sweet-smelling vagina. She let out a soft prolonged moan, as she began to grind her vagina, with coition motion around my inserted fingers. Then she slowly pushed my head from her breasts, and pulled my face to hers. She began to kiss me passionately while breathing heavy. She began to moan louder and louder. Then all of a sudden she pushed my fingers from her vagina, and stop kissing me, replying while she began to straighten her clothes on her body. "I'm sorry, baby, but we can't do this yet, you will get it, and you won't regret the wait, I promise to make up for such a frustrating night, be patient, Bobby, please, I know you think that I am a tease, but please understand me, I want you to always respect and appreciate me. Damn, we were acting like two horny teenagers on our high school prom night; at least you got your fingers wet. Don't be discourage, baby, you will get the chance to wear it out."

Before I could reply the limousine was pulling up and parking in front of her house, and as the chauffeur was opening the car's door for her, Ulrica stepped out of the car in a hurry, walking fast to her door. I had to halfway run to catch up with her, unlocking the front door to her house. Then she turned around to face me replying, "Oh, Bobby, you are such a seductive man, but not tonight, I apologize for initiating such an uncontrollable foreplay, it's my fault baby, I'm sorry everything will be alright tomorrow." Then she gave me a quick passionate kiss, before I could react, she pushed herself away from me, and stepped inside of her house replying while throwing me a kiss, "Happy New Year, baby, you will have the chance to get into me, I promise you that." She then closed her door.

I was deliriously frustrated and horny as a mother lover walking back to the limousine, smelling my fingers every now and then, the scent of my fingers caused my erection to thicken. The driver of the limousine gave me a questionable look, and I replied while getting into the passenger's section. "Driver, take me home." On my way home, I was drinking everything in the car's bar. The driver replied, "Sir, are you all right?" I replied. "Yes, it's just one of those things that just had to happen to me."

For a month and a half, I avoided seeing or talking to Ulrica, remembering what her ex-boyfriends had told me about how difficult she could be. She would call me by telephone, and I would pretend that I wasn't home, and she would leave me a message on my answer machine, apologizing for her selfish behavior on New Year day, and requesting that we have another date. I would call her house during the time of day, I knew she would be at work, stating to her answer machine, that I was busy working on a written project, and had a dead line to meet, and a date with her will interfere with my work.

I was going to different night clubs on different nights, trying to meet another attractive lady to take my mind off of Ulrica, but each night out, I did meet at least two good looking ladies, but I felt the presence of Ulrica, and the thought of her caused me to experience an impotent existence, while in the company of each of these beautiful ladies, until I met Yolanda, she was a black beauty queen who recognized me from a book, she had read that I wrote.

Yolanda and I had a heated conversation, while intoxicating ourselves at the bar of this nightclub, I just happen to wander into that nightclub which was located inside of a hotel. After acquainting ourselves with each other, Yolanda and I decided to dance, and I felt the presence of Ulrica, while holding Yolanda in my arms, dancing to a love song. She began to grind her crotch against my crotch, causing me to witness an erection, and I reciprocate the favor, copulating in slow motion. Then she whispered softly into my ear, "I don't want to be rude, but if we are going to do this, we may as well get ourselves a room, in this hotel and finish what we are doing in bed completely nude." "That sounds good to me," was what I said.

Yolanda and I checked into a room of this hotel, when she began to take off her clothes, pure gorgeous of her practically nude body showed, the feminine quality of her gender, dressed only in a thin sheer pair of bikini panties, and bra with protruding nipples of her delicious looking breasts. The sight of her body looking like that, gave me a full erection. I undressed myself to my brief, and we began a hugging and kissing foreplay technique, on each other's body like we were long lost lovers, hungry to have sex with each other.

I was kissing, licking, sucking and nipping on her lips, neck, ears, breasts and back all of that, causing her to moan from my foreplay technique. "Ah, put it in," just as I began to insert my copulating skill, between her thighs with enough agility, to cause her to experience the thrill of life. A few moments later, after I increased the movement of my copulation, she began to witness it again, multiple orgasms were causing Yolanda's moan to get louder and louder. Then the thought of Ulrica, invaded my mind, just as I was about to erupt, my sperm deep inside of her, causing me to feel guilty, and my erected penis went limp, ending our sexual experience.

I had to explain my situation to Yolanda while having breakfast with her, and she was an understanding lady. She was also cheating on her boyfriend that night, confessing that she heard that most writers were good in bed. At least I proved such rumor to be true, until I lost my erection, by then Yolanda had experienced three gratifying orgasms. She was more than satisfied with our ordeal, and the result of our experience proved that I truly loved Ulrica. After leaving the hotel, Yolanda and I gave each other a farewell kiss, and went our separate ways.

As soon as I drove into my driveway, I saw a car driving by my condominium, I only got a glimpse of the driver, and she looked a lot like Ulrica, who was gaining much respect as the new D.A. She had her workers convicting every case coming into her office. If a person was arrested for any type of crime, he or she was doing jail time or pay a regretful fine. Ulrica being as attractive as she was. She had to produce a callous attitude. Those who were guilty of white-collar crimes, she was determined for them to do some jail time. She claimed that some of the judges were discriminating against minority criminals, giving them more time to serve than the Caucasian people, who had committed the same type of crimes.

I called Ulrica on the telephone, and we talked for awhile, she been busy sending people to prison or putting pressure on her assistants to convict every case that came into her office. She talked to me in a bold way, as though she was experiencing her monthly frustration, replying impudently to me, "Look, Bobby Wilson, I like you a lot, but sometimes you piss me off, and I'm taking it out on my assistant D.A., and we are convicting a lot of people who would ordinarily get away with their criminal techniques."

My conversation with Ulrica didn't improve our relationship, so I went out again, following my womanizing desire, and met this goldish tan complexioned, blue-eyed blonde Swedish lady. She was another lady, eyes pleasing for me to see, and just as fine as she wanted to be. I was sort of skeptical about flirting with certain Caucasian women, because some of them can be downright prejudice toward dark-complexioned men, but she wasn't that type of lady at all. She approached me inquiring about my professional skill. Most professional black athletes attract women like this, and as a writer, I was giving them stiff competition.

I told her that I was a writer, and ironically, she had read books written by me. She was curious about my relationship with Creamy Caramel (Ulrica). I told her that Ulrica and I wrote a couple of books together, and that she is now a District Attorney. Joan was the name of this Swedish borne blonde, and she delighted me with a conversation of the life, she was experiencing in the United States as the owner of a large business's mistress. He allowed her to live a free single lifestyle; whenever he has to play the role of a husband to his wife, and father to their children, and since he was out of the country vacationing with his family. She was enjoying the life of a single lady while he was away.

Joan and I had a couple of drinks while we were conversing with each other, getting somewhat acquainted, and she invited me over to her house for a night of entertainment, since she was lonely and bore, I obliged her. Joan was living an affluent lifestyle in a big beautiful house. She had prepared a candle light dinner, soft music was playing on her stereo, and a bottle of French wine was chilling in a bucket of ice, to wash the food down. She had a pool table in her house.

We played a game of pool, and danced together. Joan confessed that she learned how to dance by watching television. A few more glasses of wine, and she was tipsy. I felt sort of light by the head myself. We took a seat on her couch, and watched a movie together. It was a love story, and she told me that she was lonely, and needed a man to comfort her in an intimate way, and I was the type of man who stimulated her sexual interest, before I could reply. She was kissing my lips passionately, while unfastening my shirt's buttons. How can I resist a pretty fine lady like this? We started foreplaying with each other on her couch, until we were out of our clothes. I had a mouthful of her erected Scandinavian's breast, devouring a sucking technique, while massaging her warm wet blonde vagina, then she politely pushed me away, and stood up, took me by the hand, and she lead me from her couch into her bedroombedroom, where our sexual romance began.

This was a good-looking lady in the nude, she was looking better than those women modeling in Playboy Magazine, with a cute face and a salacious body figure, nice ass, full firm breasts with erected nipples, slim waists, flat sexy stomach, long pretty legs, and a plump vagina with manicure pubic, and she was sexually experienced, now I know why this rich married man was spending big money for her honor. Joan smooth goldish tan complexion was a blessing to her appearance. Her blonde pubic was shining teasingly between her thighs, covering that stimulatingly fat piece of flesh known as her vulva.

I could tell Joan was really horny, by the way she was moaning, while she was fellatioing me, with a licking tongue and hungrily sucking lips, collaborating on my fully erected penis. Then she laid back on the bed, spreading those beautiful legs of hers, taking my erected flesh into her hand, and inserted it into her warm wet copulating vagina. I began to copulate inside her warm wet body with vibrating motions, packing her stretching vagina full of flesh, and I knew she was experiencing an orgasm by the tone of her moan. She was moaning out words I never heard before, but they were stimulating to hear, sound as though she was complimenting my prurient skill in her native language. She had me wrapped up, with her hugging arms and legs, copulating with nice firm movement, and I had her butt in the palm of my massaging hands. She was sounding so stimulating, each time she witnessed that intensified thrill of culminating joy, increasing the beats of her heart.

Just as I was about to climax another disaster happened, the thought of Ulrica entered my mind, I saw her crying, and that took all the sexual energy away from me, like a deflated tire, it went dead and fell from between her legs. I disgustedly lay to her side with tears standing in my eyes replying, "Why does this keep happening to me?"

After I told Joan about my condition of impotent, that only occurs when I'm having sex, and think about this lady Creamy Carmel. Joan began to comfort me in an understanding way, replying, "I know this can be frustrating, but at least, it allowed you the opportunity to make me feel good, and I must say it was feeling great, again and again such an ordeal like this, I will always remember." She cuddled me into her arms, while resting her head against my chest, and that the way we slept, until the next day.

We awaken and wash ourselves, before breakfast was served. Joan gave me her secret telephone number, and she had this to say. "Whenever you enhance your masculinity to resist the thought of her invading your mentality, give me a call, if you are interested, we can do this again, hoping the next time, you will witness just as good of feelings as I did, thank for such a body pleasing, heart influencing, and mind convincing romantic event, that I will always remember, and I'm quite sure, if you had experienced an orgasm, you would have fallen in love with it." I spent the rest of that day with Joan, having fun she and I, in her house alone. When I got ready to leave, I wrote her a poem, and she gave me a farewell passionate kiss, replying, "Always remember this."

A week later I called Ulrica's house, and left a message on her answering machine, because she wasn't at home. I complained to her about my situation, replying while she's out enjoying herself, dating different men with high prestige, and not feeling guilty about doing it, thoughts of her entering my mind, interrupting me, when I'm having a good time. I didn't hear from Ulrica in about two weeks, and I couldn't get with Joan, because her lover had returned home, but she would call me every now and then just to talk as friends.

Then the morning of February the fourteenth came, and my telephone began to ring, I answered it, and my heart warmed with joy, when I heard Ulrica's voice. "Bobby, I'm sorry our relationship seems to be growing thin, but tonight if you allow me, I will make it up to you. What night is better for me to prove my love for you than Valentine night itself, the holiday when true love is celebrated." My heart was invaded by such a feeling of joy, until I hardly could talk.

At nine o'clock that Valentine's night, my doorbell rung, and I answered it. There stood Ulrica with a tearful smile on her face, and a half of dozen of blue and red blending roses in her hand, extending them out to me, and she had a bag in her other hand, with a box of special made pizza, a bottle of champagne, a box of candy, and a Valentine's card. My heart was elated, when I heard she say, "Happy Valentine's, Bobby, sweetheart, I will always be your lady, and I was saving myself for this special occasion." She stepped inside my house as I took the roses and bag from her hands, and our lips connected into a prolonged wet and erection causing passionate kiss. I was loving every moment of it, while taking these items form her hands. After we finished kissing, Ulrica replied breathlessly, "Hoo-wee, Bobby, you still have that way of seducing me with your kiss. I was sort of piss off at your message about being impotent. You shouldn't try to have sex with other women, when you know, you are in love with me."

I replied while walking away to put the roses in a vase, "What am I supposed to do? You were acting like our relationship was over with or maybe your thoughts got bold, that you were stooping low, if you indulge with a Negro." Ulrica quickly defended herself against that statement. "Ethnicity got nothing to do with our relationship. Although you are the first, and only African-American, I ever dated, baby with a body and face like yours, race doesn't make a different, it's your individuality, not your ethnicity, that captivated my emotional interest, so don't come talking race shit to me, please.

I know I frustrated the hell out of you on New Year morning. I was somewhat delirious, but now that I know my feeling for you is for real, it's been years, since a man's hand or anything else about him been in that part of my body. You should consider yourself lucky, come on baby, let by gone be by gone, tonight we are going to have ourselves, some Valentine's night lovemaking fun."

Ulrica was dressed in a short red miniskirt suit, and those long pretty legs of hers, were seducing the hell out of my eyes, with an erection causing thought, as she walked pass me, going into the kitchen, and the figure of her ass in that skirt, looked just as fine as an upside down heart of Valentine's. I couldn't resist putting my hand on her behind, and giving each of her butt's cheeks a teasing squeeze. She turned around and replied, "Don't squeeze the charmer of this woman, and she might give you what you want." I replied, "Damn, baby, you look great." She replied, "I been working so hard, putting these criminals away, until I had to take time off from work, to get back in shape, and I know you will like me more looking this way."

Ulrica washed her hands in the kitchen's sink, and began to prepare the pizza for our Valentine's dinner, which had aphrodisiac toppings such as caviars, bits of fried oysters, dices green olives, bits of mushrooms, red and green peppers, Italian sausage, pepperonis and hams. This was one great tasting special made pizza, and it went fine with our glass of champagne wine, after we finished our pizza dinner, we went into the living room, sat on the couch, in front of the burning fire place, watching the romantic flame, while eating a couple pieces of this delicious tasting candy. I read my Valentine's card with an elated heart, expressing my appreciate to Ulrica for making me feel so great, and she read the card I wrote for her with tears in her beautiful eyes, sniffing once and awhile, looking at me with love in her eyes while replying, "Thank God I met you, Bobby, because you make me feel fresh and good."

Then she got up from the couch, and gave me a sweet kiss, just enough to turn on my sexual heat, and she walked toward the kitchen, to fix us something to drink, before our favorite song began to play low on my stereo. We began to slow dance. Her smooth sweet-smelling body was caressing against mine with a sexual inviting grind. I knew. I had to make impressive love to her tonight, in order to win her total existence. I would have to please her physical, emotional and mentally.

The thought came to my mind, how one of my ghetto friends describes his cunnilingus skill. When he called himself pimping women. Old Bo-dilly would describe how he would fold the tip of your tongue around his lady clitoris nice and firm, utilizing a sucking and licking technique at the same time, causing her to culminate uncontrollably. I use to laugh at Bo-dilly calling him a freak, now tonight I think I will utilize his cunnilingus skill on Ulrica as one of my ultimate foreplay technique, this would be unique, doing something that was once a taboo to me.

I started laughing at such a thought, and Ulrica replied, "What are you laughing about?" I replied, "How much I love you." I began to kiss her sweet tender lips teasingly, and she replied, "Ahh, Bobby, baby, I'm ovulating, it's a good thing, I put in my diaphragm, you will also have to use a condom mister." Then she stepped back and replied, "I want to tease you for a while." She began to take her clothes off piece by piece in a teasing way, undressing herself all the way down to her sweet-smelling sheered bikini panties and bra, full of flesh booty, crotch and breasts. Then she began to move her body with lewd seductive motion replying to me, "Bobby, my panties and bra are edible, would you like to eat them off of me?"

I said yes, and then she replied, "You would have to catch me first." She started running toward the bedroom with me chasing her. I caught up with her, pinching her seductive butt's cheeks, just as she leaped onto the bed. I dove on top of her. We started kissing each other's lips, hungrily sucking on each other's tongue. She began to undress me. Ulrica's edible panties and bra smelled like strawberry and vanilla mixed together, and they tasted delicious too.

I ate off her bra first, before devouring a mouthful of her fully erected breasts, with my lips and tongue, licking and sucking on each of them, showing each of those delicious-looking, and tasteful flesh my appreciation, before I ventured down her cute sexy stomach to her panties. While eating them off of her body, I saw that Ulrica had shaved her pubic into the shape of a heart of Valentine's, and I did an impressive job on her vagina, utilizing Bo-dilly's cunnilingus technique, causing her to culminate on my tongue again and again.

Then she asked me how would I like for her to fellatio me, I described to her the way Joan did, using her licking tongue, collaborating with her sucking lips and gum, performing a mouthful of suction, on my long erected penis, halfway down her throat, causing her to choke every now and then, but she did it with such expertise. I erupted, before I had the chance to insert into her vagina, I was so excited by the sight of her nude body, and so enthuse by the things, we were doing to each other, but I kept a marvelous hard-on.

Now it was time for me to gain more knowledge about her body, as I looked at her salacious vagina, my erection got bigger, and slowly I began to insert it into her warm, tight and wet womanhood, stretching to fit like a new pair gloves. Ulrica was practically a virgin or it has been awhile, since a penis explored her inside. I began to copulate into her body with slow screwing vibrational motion.

I was trying to impress her, with the movement of my penis, as though I was a Love Technician, with the use of it. When Ulrica began to moan, I increased my movement, and she began to moan these words into my ear. "Oh, you feel so nice inside of me." Then I put my hands under her full smooth round behind, I had each of her butt's cheeks in the palm of each hands, copulating while squeezing each of her cheek, with a massaging technique, causing her to moan louder into my ear, "Oh, you are continually feeling good! Inside of me." That when I inserted the tip of my finger into her tight wet anus, the love fluid from her vagina had flow into her anus, from the orgasms she had experienced, keeping her wet and exciting down there. The insertion of my fingertip caused Ulrica's anus and vagina to tight up with the movement of her copulating skill, and she began to breathe harder, while moaning these words into my ear. "Oh, God! Bobby, darling, you are doing such an outstandingly good fucking job, sexually pleasing me with prolonged movement, but don't think you are going to put anything else in my anus, outside the tip of your finger, that all I can handle."

I was doing all I could to impress Ulrica with my body pleasing, heart influencing and mind convincing, multiple orgasms causing technique. Her body was shivering and shaking, as each of these thrills of life lingered away, then another one would erupt, and the way she was moaning, they were erupting inside of her pretty strong. She had me wrapped up with hugging arms and legs, and we sexually enervated ourselves.

When I erupted inside of her, I collapsed on top of her, breathing loud and hard, and she rolled me off of her on my back, and she laid the side of her head against my chest, listening to the beat of my heart, while we recuperated from such an intensified sexual ordeal.

We started making love around eleven o'clock that Valentine's night in my bedroom, then we went into the Jacuzzi, from there into the shower, and back to my bedroom, doing it in different positions, I was softly biting against the flesh of her back while copulating into her vagina from behind, then she got on top of me, in a woman dominating position.

We didn't finish, until I had her in the bottom position with her butt in the palms of my hands, copulating into her pretty tough, fast and rough, trying to get another nut, and she was screaming out her moans, then I erupted inside of her pretty strong, filling her up with my sperm.

She rolled on top of me again, breathing hard with her head against my chest. Next thing I heard was Ulrica snoring into a deep sleep, and I soon joined her. It was three o'clock in the morning when we fell asleep, we awaken at eleven A.M. and we did it again, until Ulrica was too sore to do it anymore. I was sexually enervated, and had fallen deeply in love with this lady.

Since that February the fourteenth sexual experience, Ulrica and I have been indulging intimately two or three times a week. She was acting as though she's addicted to my prurient skill, introducing me to her family members, those on her Puerto Rican mother's side, and those on her Italian father's side. Ulrica spoke Spanish and Italian fluently. When she's talking to members of her Puerto Rican's family, she spoke Spanish, and would hold an Italian conversation with members of her father's family, when they came to visit her.

Most of the men on both sides of Ulrica's family showed some reluctance of greeting me, when Ulrica introduced me as her dating male friend. They considered me as a former ghetto pimp, who wrote about something, I once experienced in my life before, and they also claimed that a black man have less of a chance in profiting the quality prestige she needed, unless he's a professional athlete with outstanding skill in playing certain sport activity. They saw a rare chance for a black man to be a successful doctor, and those who were practicing law would probably sell their clients out, if they thought they could make more money from their opponents.

Ulrica boldly told her male Italian relatives off as well as she cursed out the men of her Puerto Rican's relatives for meddling in her affair, and insulting the integrity of my intelligence by judging the past history of my ethnicity, and not my individuality. I told them that I was a successful writer, and that I have written a couple of bestselling books, and that I was more a compatible mate to Ulrica's characteristic than any other male human being she had dated.

Matter of fact they got quiet, when Ulrica confessed that I was the one who inspired her to take on the advance challenge in her career. We shared the same concerned about our physical health and conscience of our hygiene. We believe in equality, that each person should be given a fair chance to prove his or her ability, and it is best for the existence of life, if a person is evaluated by his or her individuality, and not by his or her ethnicity.

Mr. Frank D'Angelo was the name of Ulrica's Italian father. He expressed his disapproval of me dating his daughter, and the fact, that I was some years older than her, and by me being a black man could put darker complexion on our children, if we decided to get marry and have a family.

Mrs. Aretha D'Angelo was the name of Ulrica's Puerto Rican mother. She was darker in complexion than her husband, and she gave us her blessing, because she once dated an African-American man in her younger days, before she met Mr. D'Angelo, and he being an affluent Italian. He brought Mrs. D'Angelo's love from this black man with the influence of his money, and she was living in poverty, moving from Puerto Rico to New York city, where she met Frank, a businessman who brought her love by giving her expensive gifts, while her black boyfriend was in the U.S. Navy stationed on ship that kept going in out to sea, and she final accepted Mr. D'Angelo's proposal to marry him.

Mr. D'Angelo's sister, Ms. Winslop who is now married to an Irishman, both have become citizen of the United States. Ms. Winslop was a flamboyant Italian woman. She was a drinker and a dancer, certainly the party type, and she admitted her admiration for me, because I reminded her of a black man she once dated, when she was a young lady, living in Naples, Italy. He was a sailor in the United States Navy. They were great lovers. He would fight the Italian men about her, and he would be winning the fight, until they gang up on him, then some of his shipmates black and white men would involve themselves in the fight, tearing up the night club, causing the owner to put his place of business off limit to U.S. servicemen.

Ms. Winslop also stated that she couldn't understand why men of other ethnicity get jealous when they see a black man from the United States dating their women, but it was all right for them to get with a black woman, especially if she's a prostitute, just to see if the rumor about black women was true, that they give a good screw.

Mr. D'Angelo interrupted his sister with this reply. "That's nonsense," Ms. Winslop continued. "Don't tell me that shit, Frank, I have seen you dating black women on different occasions." Mrs. D'Angelo replied, "Was it before or after we got married?" Mr. D'Angelo turned his attention to Ulrica replying, "Out of all of my children, you was the one, I wanted to be most successful, because you look so much like your mother with my intelligence, and by dating a man like Bobby here, no disrespect to his ethnicity, will put a dent in your reputation. This how the majority of the white people, in this country feel about Caucasian women dating black men, clandestinely they will think of you as a whore."

Ulrica got pissed off at her father, and she told him off, "I don't give a flying fuck, what those stupid people, with their ethnocentric attitudes, think of me dating him. I am a successful District Attorney, the first lady to get elected to this position, and most of my constituencies know I'm dating Bobby Wilson. Our relationship has nothing to do with our ethnicity, and for your part father, if you don't stop your stereotype attitude toward black people in this country. I don't want to see nor talk to you again, because what you are doing is a sin, and someday there will be a law, pending a criminal offense in this country against racism, no one has the right to be racial against another citizen, I'm sick of such stupidity." Mr. D'Angelo left his daughter's house a very angry man replying, "Come on, wife, let's get the hell out of here, it will snow on the equator, before I step my foot back into this house again."

Ulrica and I had given each other a key to our house, because when we go out of town for reason of business, and job related business, we could look out for each other. One week Ulrica got very sick. She got caught up with some type of flu epidemic that almost killed her. I knew, she was sick, but when I went to visit her, she was in bed couldn't move, and was having problem breathing, her fever was so high, it had sweat popping from her forehead with pain, aching from every muscle of her body. She had lost weight, and wasn't such a beautiful lady.

Ulrica was in such a life threatening condition, all I could think of was to take off my clothes, and get in bed with her, placing my forehead against her forehead, while covering her body with mine. I began to shiver and shake from such fever leaving her body, and entering into mine. I prayed in that position, until I felt asleep. That morning Ulrica awaken, feeling great her illness had gone away, she replied while smiling up at me, "You put your life on the line, just to save mine, and I love you for doing that too." I replied, "I had to do what I did, because you wouldn't have made it to the hospital, now you just stay in bed, and I will be your doctor, nurse and service."

I made breakfast for Ulrica, and serve it to her while she was in bed recuperating, and a week later Ulrica was healthy and back on her feet, doing the work of the D.A. She had to leave the state for two weeks to attend a work related meeting in Washington, D.C. with some federal officials, and I was missing her so, until one day while she was away, I received a telephone call, and it was a lady I met five years ago.

I was surprised to hear from Rosine Steven. I couldn't recognize her voice at first, but when she stalled talking about the past, to hear her voice again, I was glad. Rosine was a biracial lady African-American and Japanese. She was one of those college girls, living in my old neighborhood, who had read some of my unpublished writings, and was fascinated about my story telling talent.

When we met, I was living in this apartment complexion not too far from McChord Air Force Base in the state of Washington. Rosine's father was a black airman stationed there. He met her mother, a Japanese woman while he was stationed in Japan. He married her, and Rosine was their first borne. Some people tried to call her a war baby, but after her, they produced a family of nice looking siblings, who are now living in the United States as American citizen, and during Rosine's college stage of life, she was admired by me a lot.

On several occasions, I tried to seduce her, when she dressed herself up on the weekends, her award winning, stimulating appearance, brought so much pleasure to my intoxicated eyes. I would compliment her with words of lust, causing her to blush, but she would refuse me with these words. "No, Bobby, but if you become a successful writer, I promise to indulge intimately with you, for putting forward such a diligent effort to be successful.

Rosine told me why she decided to call me up, and I could tell by the sound of her voice, that her conversation was pertaining to that proposition; she had made me back then. Now she was an officer in the Air Force, serving as a pilot, flying jet fighter warplanes, she also told me, she had read every books I have published, and since she was visiting this area, she found my name in the telephone book, and decided to give me a call, requesting to stop by my resident, and reminisce a bit.

I told her okay that sound admiring to me, and I was about to give her the direction to my house, when she replied, "That's alright, I know where you stay. I'm only two blocks away, I'll be there in ten minutes, see you later." After I hung up the telephone, within ten minutes, my door's bell rung. I answered the door, and there Rosine stood, dressed in her Air Force uniform, with the rank of captain, showing on her shoulders and cap. I could tell that she was military orientated, because she was there exactly ten minutes.

She was glad to see me, and we embraced each other with hearts warming and bodies caressing hugs, then she gently kissed my lips replying afterward, "Wow, Bobby, it is so good, to see my old womanizing friend again, and mister successful writer, you are looking better with age. Success has really rejuvenated you." I stared at her with an agape look on my face replying, "Rosine, this is you, wow, you are looking militarily matured good, come inside, and tell me about your life."

Rosine and I had a drinking conversation, while I prepared a meal for us to eat. She was sitting at the kitchen's bar admiring me with words of flirting compliment, and I expressed my appreciation to her for making me feel great. Then she interrupted me with questions about the lady who has conquered my emotional interest, so I told her about Ulrica and her career.

Rosine replied, "Well, I'm jealous of her, and it's a good thing, she's out of town, so let's have a good time for old time sake, since you are a successful writer, and I'm doing good as a commissioned officer in the Air Force, a female military officer and a male writer, what a combination, I promise not to hesitate, if you want to go all the way, reacquainting ourselves with each other."

I thought before putting a smile on my face. "It's a good thing, I brought some condoms, because I was feeling kind of horny the last two days, and Rosine was a salacious looking lady in her military dress uniform, and the sight of her legs were turning me on."

Rosine gave me a shy sexual look, as though she was reading my mind. Then she replied, "You know, Bobby, I must confess, even back then, I was reluctant to let you know this, when you use to flirt with me, you possessed such a sexual stimulating personality, causing the erection of my breasts nipples and clitoris to stiffen, making me witnessed such a sensational feeling.

"Until it was intimidating for me to be in the company of you alone, and on several occasions, I went off by myself, and masturbated, imagining how great it would feel, having you pack your hard moving flesh inside of me, back then you had the intuition of a pimp, and the thought of me having sex with you, had me getting off on my fingers tips, so I decided back then, one day 1 was going to build up enough courage to my womanhood, and have sex with you, but somehow we went our separate ways.

"I have had sex with other men, of course they were my boy-friends, who I had dated occasionally, and while having sex with each, I would imagine, they were you, then I began to feel real good, experiencing that thrill of life, so intensified, until I began to cry, because it wasn't my date, making me feel that great. It was my imagination of your sexual play, and I'm here to cure this sexual phobia, I have for you, hee-hee life can be so mysterious, hah, Bobby Wilson."

I replied, "You mean to tell me that you were evading my horny attempt, to seduce you back then, and after those years, of using your imagination to create a thoughtful feeling, of having sex with me, while indulging intimately with your date, made you feel sexually great, now you want to have sex with me to cure your curiosity. I appreciate your seduction, and I'm oblige you with some good loving."

I tried to act like a gentleman for a while, being conservative as her host, but I'm only a man with gentleman's ways, and after she told me what her interest was, it would be rude of me, to turn down this beautiful lady, in such a seductive mood. Rosine became too stimulating for me to resist her seducing kisses.

We started off by slow dancing to a love song. We had each other wrapped caressingly close with cuddling arms, while the crotches of our bodies were grinding against each other. She began to whisper salacious words into my words, while copulating her crotch against mine. We were in my living room, dancing in front of the fireplace, watching the reflection of ourselves in the big mirror over the fireplace.

Rosine was too persistent for me to resist her sexual invasion, and we ended up, encountering a romantically intimate rendezvous on the couch of my living room, in front of the fireplace, which brought stimulating heat to our sexual performance. After Rosine totally undressed herself, neatly folding her uniform and placing it on the recliner, and we went at each other like lust puppies, licking and sucking hungrily on each other body, before the insertion, and she welcomed me, warm and wetly, copulating as though we were in competition trying to out screw one another, and I love it, when a woman moves her body, during sexual intercourse with me.

I lost all thoughts of stop pumping, my fully erected flesh, inside of her warm wet and welcoming vagina. I sexually gave her what she came there for, an outstanding body pleasing performance, from my foreplay technique, to my copulating skill, her vagina was full of moving flesh, accelerating long, hard and deep into her body motion, that started off slow, and she moaned into my ear, "Oh, Bobby, baby, give me more you are making me feel so ggooodd."

It was breathtaking for her to culminate into such intensified multiple orgasms, each of her body pleasing thrill, erupted from deep inside the walls her vagina, influencing her emotion with each beat of her heart, convincing her mind that she was having a damn good time. I had to increase the speed of my movement in order for me to experience such thrill of life, and she started calling me God, telling me how good it was feeling to her, and my movement got rougher like a trifle lover, and she seen to be enjoying it more, when I began a crawling copulation technique between her smooth yellowish-brown thighs, the pain was just enough, to make Rosine erupt, into another prolonged moan, and I started huffing and puffing, while experiencing such a thrilling orgasm with hers.

As we lay on the couch sexually enervated, breathing more calmly while enjoying the lingering of such a thrill, Rosine began to kiss my lips replying, "After all these years, you finally prove to me, that you are a penis technician, and I enjoyed your expertise, yes indeed." I replied, "Thank you, baby, and I enjoyed the hell out of you too."

Then the thought of Ulrica crossed my mind, and I began to rush Rosine to wash up, because I had a feeling that Ulrica was back in town, and she was coming my way. Rosine and I took a shower together. She began to play around with me while we were getting dressed. She was trying to cause me to receive another erection. After we got dressed, I was walking Rosine to her car, and Ulrica drove up. I introduced Rosine to Ulrica, and she told Ulrica, she was the luckiest woman in this world to have a man with my quality of love.

Rosine boldly walked up to me, and gave me a farewell hug and a gentle kiss on my lips, before she walked away, getting into her car. Then she spoke to Ulrica before driving off. "Your competition is getting thick, if I was you, I will marry him quick, and I salute you for controlling his emotional interest, because he really loves you, and that is plain to see."

After Rosine drove away, Ulrica gave me a tearful stare. I saw anger in her beautiful bluish-green eyes. As we walked into the house, Ulrica kept straight to the bar, and she poured herself a small glass full of Wild Turkey whiskey. I knew. I was in trouble, when I saw Ulrica drank all that whiskey, down in one big groaning swallow. Ulrica surprised me, when she spoke ghetto bold. "I'm about to become, an ass-kicking whore, and I ain't bullshitting neither."

I walked into the living room, trying to think of something to say, that would sooth the emotion of this angry D.A., and I almost holler from fright, when I saw Rosine's panties laying on the floor, showing itself halfway, under the corner of the couch. I quickly stepped toward them with such agility, giving them a stiff kick, forcing them farther under the couch, where they couldn't be seen, and thinking to myself, "That bitch ass Rosine, left her motherfucking panties here on purpose, damn conniving whore, trying to get me in trouble with my lover."

Ulrica was walking toward the living room, while I walked pass her, going into the kitchen, to get me a beer from the refrigerator, and while I was walking back toward the living room I replied, "So how was life in Washington, D.C. what wrong with you, I don't get a hug and kiss, you been gone for two weeks." Ulrica replied boldly, "You fuck that slut ass bitch, posing as a military officer turning tricks, didn't you mister horny ass, Bobby 'penis technician' Wilson."

I replied while walking by her into the living room, "No, I didn't, don't be ridiculous with such mendacious accusation." Ulrica became bodacious with her abusive language. "You are a lying son-of-a-bitch, and I don't mean to put your mother into this, but motherfucker! Who in the hell! You think. You are fucking with. I believe in monogamy. When I became your lover, you promised to only have sex with me, mister lying pimp ass Negro. You don't fuck no other whore, after indulging with me intimately, do you hear me, Bobby Wilson."

Before I could speak, she gave me a hard painful and frustrating slap, against the back of my head, and that irritated the hell out of me: mental, emotional and physically. I lost my cool, and I was about to act a fool replying, "What is fucking wrong with you, just because you spend two weeks in Washington, D.C., cheating on me, with those big time affluent politicians, don't come back here, taking your guilt trip out one me, because I'm not taking, no kind of bull shit from you, and you best keep your got- damn hand to yourself."

Ulrica let out a prolonged scream as she shouted out, "I dare you to accuse me of doing something, you just did, mister infidelity, I maybe a cute faced lady with a fine physical shape, but I be got-damn, if I'm going to pull my panties down, and mess around with every Tom, Dick and Harry in town, I'm too intelligent for that type of bull shit, hhooo, you are pissing me off mister." All of a sudden Ulrica grabbed me by my shoulder, and snatched me around to face her, and before I could say a word, I felt a stinging pain, from her opened hand, slapping against my face. A couple of her fingers hit me in my eye, turning my light out, momentarily blinding me.

She really pissed me off then. I grabbed both of her shoulders, and gave her a frustrated shake, jerking her body. Ulrica let out another irritating scream, while bringing both of her arms up, knocking my hands from her shoulders. Before I could react, I was under her physical attack. She forced her knee against my crotch, the pain from it, folded me over, taking my breath away, then she hit me with her fist, a hard upper cup against my chin, lifted me up, as I was staggering backward, trying to gain my composer. Ulrica maneuvered her body with such physical agility, throwing combination of jabs against my face, knocking me to the floor on my back.

As I rolled over to get up, on my hands and knees, Ulrica screamed out these words. "You pussy-loving motherfucker! When you are making love to me, you fuck no other bitch, do you hear me, mister pimp ass Negro, and I don't mean to insult your ethnicity. I'm not going to be, another one of your fucking whores." Then she gave me a hard kick against my rib's cage, with enough force to send me rolling on the living room floor, I was hollering, while she kicked and brutalized my body.

I became infuriated replying, "Ahh, got damn, you are trying to kill me, I'm call the police, fuck this bullshit, and it's time for one to retaliate." Ulrica stepped back in her self-defense stand, in front of the couch, shouting these words out. "Retaliate! That what I want you to do, come on with it, and the consequent will be detrimental to your motherfucking health!"

Before she knew it, I was off the floor, back on my feet, evading each punch and kick, she tried connect against me, but she was missing, because I was weaving and bobbing, ducking and dodging them, while maneuvering, and quickly I advanced in on her, grabbing a handful of her face, palming it like a basketball. I gave her face a hard push, with enough force to send her body, backward against the couch, flipping over it. Ulrica let out a painful scream, as she was falling over the couch, her legs opened, showing off her black sheer panties, before she hit the floor.

She lay there screaming as though she was going insane. "Ahheee, I'm kick your good fucking ass now!" She jumped to her feet with all of her fingers' nails pointing at me. She came clawing at me, with kicking feet, barely missing me. I turned to run, and she ripped my shirt from my body. I hauled ass, running toward the bedroom, and she chased me there.

As soon as I entered the bedroom, Ulrica caught up with me, grabbing me from behind, I quickly turned around, ducking her swinging fist. I quickly maneuvered around her, forcing both of her hands to her side, locking my arms around her body in that position. Then I lifted her, and carried her to the bed. She was kicking her legs replying, "Let go of me, and fight fair like a human being, prove your gender, mister don't be cheating, I'm kick your ass fair fisted. What the matter? You afraid, coward son-of-a-bitch, let go of me. Is this the only way you can win, by using your strength, to hold me in this position hah."

I felt on the bed with her locked in my arms, and I held her there, locking my legs around hers, I was behind her, speaking nice and slow, words of confident, trying to be convincing to hear. We both were exhausted, and I was hurting the most. "Wow, baby, what is wrong with you, kicking my ass, for something I didn't do. Ulrica, you know I love you, and I always will, that's the truth. Now I know what your ex-friend was talking about you being a wild cat."

Ulrica replied, "That Jeff Wright don't know what the fuck he's talking about, a lying white son-of-a-bitch, I never had sex with him. When I was a freshman in college, that bastard tried to date rape me, during my monthly cycle, I was doing some heavy bleeding, he didn't care, he just want to have sex, little did he knew, I could fight like hell too. I physically kicked his ass, had his eyes, nose and mouth bleeding, I put his got-damn face on a period, and he begged me not to tell his friends."

I replied, "Okay, that was in the past, now I know that you can kick ass, but meeting you, I'm still glad." Ulrica interrupted me, speaking impudently. "Fuck this shit, turn me a loose, so I can go home, Bobby, I do love you, but we are through, I'm acting like a silly ass concubine, with a nincompoop's attitude, I'm not cohabiting with you anymore, our fornicating relationship is over with. This love, that I have for you, got me acting a jealous hearted fool. I'm have to stop seeing you."

Ulrica started crying, and I continued expressing my love for her, talking pleasingly, while she cried herself to sleep, and I fell asleep with her body locked between my legs and arms. We slept in that position, until morning came. Ulrica awaken in a calm way. She spoke nice and apologetic to me. "Good morning, Bobby darling, I apologize for acting so jealous and wild, yesterday, but you know how to calm the anger of a lady."

I groaned as I moved to release her. "Oh, baby, you tried to kill me." She replied, "No, darling, if I wanted to kill you, I could have done that easily, when you get a chance, look into my purse, and you will see, what I'm talking about, but my heart wouldn't let me, do anything pernicious to you. I wanted to take your body through, what I was feeling, hurt, when I saw you and Ms. Air Force Slut, coming from this house with an 'I just fuck your man smile on her face.' I appreciate you for lying all the way, denying every bit of my accusation. I had no proof, so you won this case, and I still love you."

I rolled away from Ulrica, groaning from the pain, she had bruised my body with, and I went to my bedroom's dresser, opened a draw, and pulled out a jewelry box. I brought the jewelry box to the bed, where Ulrica was lying, with an amazing smile on her face. I got down on my knee beside the bed, facing Ulrica, replying to her, while opening the jewelry box. "If it not too late, Ulrica will you marry me, please, I promise to be a great husband." At that moment, I opened the jewelry box, and the bright sparkle from the diamond ring, flashed into Ulrica's eyes. It brought tears of joy to her eyes, and she began to cry while replying.

"Oh, Bobby, that is a beautiful ring, and yes of course, I will marry you, may as well, I'm madly in love with you."

This ring was customer made, designed by me from a dream, I had, and I asked the jeweler to make it, like a puzzle wedding set of a heart shape, with diamonds inserted into the heart shaped gold, and the other part of this set, was a ring with a star shaped diamonds, that goes into the heart of the other's ring like a puzzle. As I was placing the ring on her finger, Ulrica's lips met mine, and we sealed this proposal with a I love you forever-passionate kiss. As our lips parted, Ulrica replied, "Thank you, Lord, my God and Jesus Christ, for blessing me to meet, and about to marry, the man of my desire, Bobby Wilson, I promise to be a great wife to you, until the day I die."

Then I presented her with another gift, replying, "Here is something to wear on that special day like our wedding day. The sight of a pearl necklace set, with a pendant of a praying angel in flight. The body of this angel was made of gold. The wings were made of pearls, and the head of this angel was made of a diamond. There was a pair of earrings, matching the pendant of this pearl necklace.

Ulrica replied, "Oh my God, Bobby, this is gorgeous, I want you to know, we will never fight again, like we did last night or like I did, you were just trying to defend yourself, and I don't blame you baby, but I'm curious, did it took an ass kicking, before you proposed to me." I replied, "No, I was just waiting for the right moment, and Rosine unannounced visit showed me something about you, I don't want to witness again. Understanding is the best thing in this world, between two people who are in love, from now on, let's compromise through a conversation, that's the best way to negotiate, now let's promise each other, that we will never go to bed angry at one another."

The pain of my bruised body began to ach, and I replied, "I'm going to sit in the Jacuzzi for a while." Ulrica gave me a tender passionate kiss, before she replied, "I'm sorry, baby, for hurting you, and I deeply appreciate the tactic you used to prevent yourself from physically abusing me. I'm wash up a bit, before fixing us something to eat, then I will be there, to soothe all of your aching pain away, with my unique massaging technique."

I was relaxing in the stimulatingly heated water of the Jacuzzi. All of a sudden, I began to hear some music of soulful songs by Al Green and Aretha Franklin, playing on the stereo, filling the house with the sound of loving soul, warming my heart emotionally firm, by the words of these songs. "Love and Happiness" Al Green was sounding so convincing, and then a song by Aretha Franklin began to play. It had my heart thinking mentally, with a thoughtful feeling. "I never loved a man the way I love you."

When I looked up, while sitting in the Jacuzzi, I saw my wife to be, Ulrica walking toward me, dressed in a sheer sexy green grown. She had some of her clothes here at my house, just in case she wanted to cohabitate with me over the weekend, her grown was opened at the front, revealing her see through green panties and bra. She was holding a tray of food in her hands replying, "How about breakfast in the Jacuzzi, my husband to be."

After we ate breakfast, we drank a glass of Gin mixed with orange juice, and before we knew it; we were in a sexual mood. Ulrica gave me a muscle relaxing massage, stimulating my sexual interest, and I received an erected penis. I was filled with so much sexual enthusiastic, until I began to breath warmly through my nose against the flesh of her soft tender smooth neck, creating such a sexual sensation, causing the nipples of her breasts to stiffen, with stimulating erection, looking so delicious protruding against the material of her sheer bra. Little did I knew this foreplay technique had stimulated the area of her vagina with a sexual itch, erecting her clitoris, while heating up the walls of her vagina, with the warm moist of her body's fluid.

I was ready to go inside of her beautiful smooth thighs, where the thrill of her paradise lies, awaiting me to enter her with copulating and vibrating movement, starting off nice and slow, ending up fast and rough, trying to get a nut, that when my orgasm erupted. This technique was intriguing for Ulrica to witness such a fascinating thrill.

We started off raw in the Jacuzzi, then we ended up in my bed, enough been said, we got so intimately involved, sexually pleasing each other, until Ulrica paused for a moment to call her job, telling them that she won't be coming in today, and we played husband and wife, throughout that day and the most of that night.

A month later, Ulrica awaken one morning, with a certain nauseated feeling, sending her to the bathroom, and throwing up her food. She was reluctant to get upset, because she knew the result of such sickness, and she was skeptical about the condition she was in, so immediately, she took a home pregnancy test, and the result of it, proved that she was positively pregnant, with an ambiguous attitude, about what she was going to do. She called me, because she was confused, asking me why I didn't use a condom, when we were indulging intimately, and I replied, "Because I thought you were using contraceptive, when we were making love together, beside I remembered several times, while we were in the thick of doing it, you took the condom off of me."

Ulrica spoke with a smile on her face. "Okay, I'm the guilty party, bare flesh feel the best, I must confess, having your warm hard bare flesh moving inside of me, filling the walls of my vagina stretchingly, it does be feeling good, to think about it right then and there, and besides, I didn't want to have sex that day anyway. I wanted to kick your ass, for fucking around with Rosine, that Air Force bitch, while you supposed to be in love with me, after you proposed, my emotion warmed my body in a sexual way." I replied, "We have to get married, before your pregnancy began to show. What would it look like, the District Attorney showing up at work pregnant, with an illegitimate child."

On June the 19ᵗʰ, two thousand and five, Ulrica became my wife. This date has something to do with the significance, pertaining to the official freedom of the United States' slaves, and we agreed to get marry on that day. The sun was shining, and the wind was blowing a cool breeze of air everywhere. Our wedding ceremony was held at this well-known Catholic Church. I have visited there on several occasions, while dating Ulrica, and she would also visit the United Methodist church with me, because of my obligation to that particular religious denomination.

Mr. Frank D'Angelo reluctantly escorted his daughter Ulrica to the altar, offering her to me, under his shy reluctance, to be the lady, who will share her life with me, until death do us apart, at least that the way it supposed to be, and my ex coworker, Sal Lombar, who told me about Ulrica, when she was an attorney at law, working on my plagiaristic case. She found those who were guilty, and the rest was history. After that we started dating, and that is why, I chose Sal to be my best man, dressed in his tuxedo, standing next to me, whispering these words out to me. "I can't believe, what I'm seeing, and I will get the chance to kiss Mrs. Ulrica D'Angelo-Wilson's lips as your best man, thank you again Bobby Wilson for choosing me to do this."

Our wedding reception was held at Ulrica's resident, most of her relatives were living in that region of the United States, and some of them had spouses of different ethnicities. I had chartered a flight for my mother, and her choice of my sisters, brothers, nieces, nephews, cousins and other relatives, plus a few of my childhood friends, to attend the wedding of Ulrica and me, and each of them was welcomed to invite a spouse or a friend.

There were a lot of people at our wedding reception, greeting us as married couple, and there were plenty of food, music and drinks, everyone was having a good time laughing, talking and dancing with each other. People from different class of living were represented, at our wedding reception, in and outside the house, from the richest and the intellect, to the poor, and those who had little or no education. There were people hired to do the cooking, cleaning and waiting on our guests, while the security people operated the video cameras, in and outside the house. They also walked around among the guests for the safety of them.

Ulrica and I were together, greeting family members, guests and friends, receiving their blessings with hands shakes from the men and hugs and kisses from the women, taking pictures together with them. Members of Ulrica's family, most of them congratulated us with good wishes, welcoming me to their family, nothing like an in-law of a different ethnicity. A few members of Ulrica's family gave us that impudent look, which we over looked.

Ulrica's niece caught the bouquet of flowers that she tossed over her head backward, into a crowd of single women, waiting to catch it, and her father spoke in a low voice. "I hope she doesn't many a man of his ethnicity." That remark was ignored by the people cheering her victory, and my cousin Archie caught the garter, I slide teasingly down Ulrica's long beautiful leg, men at the reception made a wooing sound, at the sight of them, when I raised her wedding dress, to pull down the garter belt, and threw it over my head backward into a crowd of men, trying to catch it, and cousin Archie out jumped them, and caught it, bringing it to his nose, smelling it and grinning.

When Ulrica and I went to greet my family members, she ran to my mother with hugging arms, and kissing lips on her cheek, replying, "Thank you for coming to our wedding, Ms. Wilson, and a special thank to you for giving birth to my husband. He means so much to me: Mental, emotional and physically." My mother replied, "I'm happy for you two, my son Bobby Ray, finally met his Miss Pulchritudinous, the lady of his dream, and I sense from the look of you, I'm about to have a grandchild soon."

Ulrica gave my mother a blushful smile before replying, "Yes, Ms. Wilson, you are a very wise woman, and I'm not even showing, you see your son, and I were having too much fun, without a condom on, but anyway, it brought on our wedding day, and I'm proud to be your daughter-in-law." My mother replied, "And I'm proud to have you as my daughter-in-law too, Mrs. Ulrica Wilson, we welcome you to this family with loving hearts."

Later on that day, during the reception, night was invading day; most of the people had enjoyed themselves, expressed their appreciations and congratulations, and were going their separate ways, leaving behind some family members of Ulrica and mine. I was off in a corner, talking with some of my nephews and brothers, when that Clyde Jr. a corrupted nephew of mine, confronted me with an altercation, talking ghetto impudently, expressing his jealousy of my success.

Clyde Jr. was in his usual drugged up intoxicated mood, staggering up to me, mumbling out these words, trying to start a fight. "Bar Ray boy, I never did like your bitch ass anyway. I have to beg Big Mama, to let me come here with her, so I can fuck, your punk ass up." Another one of my nephew, Charles spoke out. "Ah, Clyde Jr., you shouldn't be talking to your uncle like that, especial on his wedding day."

Clyde Jr. spoke out boldly again. "Fuck uncle, that nigger's just a few years older than me, we damn near grew up together, he use to whip my ass, when I was little, but now I'm bigger than him, payback is a motherfucker. I was feeling good. When he finished college, and couldn't find a job, didn't had a woman, no money, no car, living back home with Big Mama, then all of a sudden this motherfucker, come to this state, and got lucky enough, to meet this rich white lady, who had what it takes, to bring success his way. You are one N————, I hate."

I tried to keep my cool, knowing that Clyde Jr. came to my wedding, just to act a fool, little did I knew at that moment, Ulrica and one of her relative were also debating in an unfriendly way. She slapped her cousin's face, and sent her away. Now my nephew is acting a fool with me. I replied to his remark. "She is not white, she's an Italian-Puerto Rican American, and her ethnicity has nothing to do with our relationship. It's all about our individualities, and compatibilities, also I'm tire of you trying to insult me."

Clyde Jr. staggered closer to me, mumbling out his words. "Ah, Negro, don't try to get intellectual with me, I don't care what she is, she still a Caucasian. Why you couldn't marry a black lady? Nigger, I ought to spit, in your motherfucking face, grew up fucking black women, all your poor ass life, now you got some money, you up and marry a white woman." I became infuriated, from what I heard Clyde Jr. said, I was about to become ghetto rude, replying. "Fool, if you spit in my face, today will be your dying day, I will bird gut, your got damn fool acting ass, cutting you from your asshole, all the way up to your motherfucking throat. I'm calling your bluff. I have had sex with women of different nationalities, and ethnicities, while I was in the navy, going to different places of this world, and everywhere I went, there was no black women."

My brother intervened replying to my nephew, "Look, Clyde Jr., why don't you be cool, and stop acting like a drunk ass fool, there are all kinds of people, marrying into this family, you had a chance to marry a lady, with just as much prestige, but you let that dope get the best of you." Clyde replied, "Nah, this nigger, talking about cutting me, I'm from the penitentiary, use your fist nigger, I'm about to whip that tuxedo off your ass, I don't give a damn about none of you Wilson boys."

I was ready to fight. My nephew had frustrated me, on my wedding night, and I replied. "You are a lying switching bitch, you were in and out of prison, because you have a boyfriend there, packing your butt with flesh." I turned to walk away, that was when Clyde made his attack, swinging his fist, trying to hit me from behind. I saw him coming up on me from the corner of my eye, and I reacted with such agility, causing him to miss. I weaved and bobbed with such maneuverability, while Clyde tried to grab me. I landed a hard hooking jab against his rib cage, afflicting enough pain upon impact, causing him to holler, weakening his knees.

He was about to collapse to the ground, but I gave him a quick hard upper cup against his chin, lifting him up off his feet, then I sort of side stepped him, while he was staggering backward. I threw a fast straight jab, my fist collided between his eyes, turning his light out, salvia flew from his mouth, as he began to snore, while falling to the ground, knock out cold, unconscious, with a bleeding nose. Whenever members of my family get together for some type of event, inevitably there will be some type of altercation, leading into a physical conflict caused by jealousy.

That incident interrupted some other activities, going on as a part of this wedding reception, and my youngest brother Lumpy replied,

"Bobby, you did the right thing to that fool, ass nigger coming to your wedding reception, just to clown you. I would have knocked his ass out too." Lumpy gave Clyde Jr. a kick against his butt, before pouring some beer into his face, waking him up. After Clyde Jr. regained his conscience, he began to apologize. "Ah, Uncle, you knew I was drunk, you didn't have to dog me out like that, knocking me out in front of these people."

Ulrica came to the scene replying, "Oh, no, this is a shame, Bobby darling, did you have to do your nephew like this." Security people arrived on the scene, while Ulrica assisted Clyde Jr. to his feet. He felt ashamed, sniffing back his tears replying, "Ah, man, I'm sorry for acting a fool at your wedding, I was high off that stuff, and once again, I apologize for everything." Ulrica, speaking to calm his embarrassed attitude. "That all right, Clyde Jr., everybody gets uptight, every once and awhile in their lives, you are still welcome to our house, by the way darling, we best get ready for our honeymoon cruise."

During our honeymoon cruise, I was once again, sailing on the high sea, not as a sailor, doing my military duties, but as a man, married to the lady of my desire, giving praise to my lord and savior Jesus Christ, sailing under a full moon of this dark sky. This was a huge ocean liner with all the ingredient of a floating city.

Hawaii was the first place we visited, going to different places, doing things together just as Ulrike had planned, traveling as spouses, enjoying this tropical paradise, sightseeing and shopping for different souvenirs. I usually walk with my hand in my pocket for the purpose of our safety, and Ulrica would walk beside me, holding on to my arm. We were catching all kind of attentions, not as newlyweds, but as two unique looking human beings, physically pleasing to see of different gender and ethnicity. I was some years older than Ulrica, but physically, we were made for each other.

At night before going to bed, we got on our knees, beside our bed, and prayed together, then our state room neighbor would hear the sound of intimate moan, coming through the wall of our state room, from us having sexual fun, enjoying life as newlyweds can be so sensation, if the husband and wife, loved one another like we loved each other, not lust, but mental, emotional and physical love, pleasing each other total existence,

The next day we went about our business, greeting different people, living aboard this cruise ship, participating in the different activities, organized by the public relation department of this ship, as this luxurious ocean liner cruised from Hawaii, heading toward Mexico. A few days touring there, then we went through the Panama Canal, visiting places like the Virgin Island, Jamaica, and Puerto Rico, also visited some of Ulrica's family members on her mother side, still living there.

Ulrica had taken a month leave of absence from her job, and her subordinates knew how to get in touch with her, if an emergence occurs, requiring her expertise. They could get in touch with her through this ocean liner communication system. Ulrica and I started what we called our bedroom conference, something advisable for every husband and wife to do, known as spouse commitment, verbally communicating before going to sleep, if we are not exhausted from indulging in a prolonged intimate ordeal.

We would discuss different situations while lying in bed, negotiating in a compromising way, instead of debating the issue, she would talk and I would listen, commenting on what I heard, then she would listen, while I elaborate. This type of conversation was better after we indulge sexually. We agreed not to go asleep angry at each other, so far no conflict like that, have occurred between us yet. Ulrica talked about being in the position, to do something for the poor and common people like assisting them to get in a better position in life.

She was concern about people living in the ghettoes, the homeless, youth gangs, illegal drugs users, racism, homosexuality, and what it would take to turn the United States into a nation that practice true democracy. She wanted to see equality distributed among all U.S. citizens, and the civil right law protects us all. I knew from our conversation. I was married to a lady with political obligation, and the determination to become the type of politician, with such prestige to make national decisions, affecting the lives of all citizens.

One night we were wrestling around in the bed, inventing new ways to stimulate each other as foreplay, before making love. I would act like a Vampire or a wild animal, attacking her with biting teeth, just enough pressure to stimulate her sexual interest. While lying in each other's arms, I thought about the way she physically attacked me, and asked her who taught her how to fight so diligent and detrimentally.

She told me that her father enrolled her in a martial art school at a young age, because she was small and cute. He didn't want her to be bullied by the other children. She confessed, that she grew up with a shy tomboyish attitude. She would always get into fights with her brothers and cousins. Ulrica replied, while lying in my arms, looking at the ceiling of our stateroom, "Bobby, the thought of that night, we fought, about that bitch Rosine, making me jealous, I shouldn't call her that, because if it wasn't for her, coming into the picture, I wouldn't be wearing this ring, and your name, Mrs. Ulrica D'Angelo-Wilson."

I replied, "Ah, let's forget about that incident." Ulrica replied, "I have something to say anyway, if you had hit me, the way you punched out your nephew Clyde Jr. I would have shot you, and I knew you looked into my purse, and saw my 380 automatic pistol, but you handled that situation like a gentleman, beautifully, you held me, until I cried myself to sleep. I love you for doing that." I replied, "Have you ever lost a fight?" She replied, "You had to ask, hell yeah, she was a black girl, attending the same Jr. high school as I. She was on the girl boxing team, plus she worked out with weight."

Ulrica paused for a moment, then she continued. "She was built fine with muscles, and I admired her, to be a female, she was a hunk, and the way we got into this fight. I was taking up for my little red neck Tennessee hillbilly friend, named Henry Jean, and Odessa was the name of this black girl, who was walking by, while Henry Jean and I were outside talking. Henry Jean used the 'N' word, and Odessa heard her."

Odessa replied, "Oh, no, I did not hear, this little red neck, cracker faced, pecker wood bitch, use the word nigger, did I, are you talking to me bitch!" Before Henry Jean could say anything, Odessa had punched against her face with her fist, knocking Henry Jean unconscious to the ground. That when I jumped in, with my feet, kicking Odessa against her head, and we fought like pros, and I ended up with a black eye and a bloody nose, but Odessa's body and face were bruised too. That was the only time, I can remember, getting defended by another female human being.

I gave Ulrica a cuddling hug, embracing her with caressing arms, replying, "Damn, she blackens my baby's eye." Ulrica replied, "Ah, man, a whole lot of racism shit, broke out from that incident. My brothers and cousins went to seek revenge. They were going to beat up on Odessa, and Odessa's family members and friends ambushed them. They ended up having a big racial gang fight. The police had to intervene. Our parents had to come to meetings with us at school, as a community effort to end racial problems, occurring among their youth, that when Odessa and I became the best of friends, throughout our Jr. high school years. I went to a private high school, only a few black students went there."

Our honeymoon tour gave us a chance to visit Barcelona, Spain. Those African-Spanish women were eyes pleasing to see physically. Ulrica stay close to me, as we went about our business, enjoying the life of this great city, before we were on the ship again, visiting places around the Mediterranean Sea such as: Athens, Greece; Naples, Italy; Ulrica had some relatives living there, who we also visited, and saw some black ex-military men from the United States, living in the neighborhood of Ulrica's relatives, who had married Italian women, and decided to live in Italy.

From Naples, Italy, we went on a tour with a group of people to Roman, visiting the palace of Julius Caesar. We even visited a theatre there, to see a play of Caesar assassination. From Italy across the Mediterranean, we visited the city Tunis of Tunisia, Africa next door to Algeria to experience the taste of African culture.

We visited Paris, France, this was an expensive honeymoon, Ulrica wanted to go through the tunnel, Princess Diana of England lost her life in, then from Paris to London, England, before heading back to the United States, pulling into the port of New York City, from there we flew across the United States to Portland, Oregon.

Ulrica's pregnancy was more noticeable by her associates and colleagues, when we returned home from our honeymoon, their remarks were. "Wow, that was quick, you got pregnant in a few weeks, your husband is full of fertility." She also received some unappreciated commits from some of her male Caucasian friends. "Ulrica, you are looking nice, but I can't believe my eyes, you really married that black guy, and went on your honeymoon, returning home with your stomach showing, filled with his unborn. Meaning, you are about to give birth to his child. There must be some type of social illness, spreading throughout the United States, call Negro-Caucasian, that when white women lost their minds, and give birth to black babies."

Ulrica got upset with those remarks, and began to excogitate on a way to eliminate racism in the United States, and as a pregnant District Attorney, she was putting forward her best effort to cut down racial crime rate. She attacked the Justice Department, claiming that they were showing discrimination in its system against minority people, when it comes to sentencing those who were found guilty of the crimes they committed.

She discovered that people of the minority, especially black people, who committed the same type of crime, that the people of the Caucasian race committed, but by being dark, their ethnicity seems to cause them to receive more incarcerated time, and a heavier fine, showing bias toward their existence, accusing them of being inferior people, but reality is proving the different, preventing equality from being distributed.

Ulrica wanted to investigate the reason why most state's prison has a high percentage of black inmates. She thought there were some unjust dealing by the justice system, to keep a certain amount of black people in an inferior position, causing them to lose their citizenship, for the crimes they committed, in and out of prison, once they were freed, no place to go, but back to the ghetto, lost their right to vote, keeping the wrong politicians in such a position, to under mind their existence.

Ulrica was a lover of equality, and wanted each citizen of this country to receive candid treatment by the justice system. As District Attorney, Ulrica created a special task force to investigate people working for the

Justice Department, utilizing the positions they were in, to receive bribes to discriminate against certain people or misuse their positions as a get rich scheme, and she had a couple of top law enforcing officials, a few city's politicians, and three judges under such surveillance.

These people were on the verge of losing their jobs, by underestimating the position Ulrica was in, as the District Attorney, with the authority to have any person arrested, and convicted for breaking the law, that was written to be enforced, and for each citizen to abide by.

These laws were the guidance to their everyday living, forbidding them to do things against these regulations, and those people in certain authoritarian positions, committing certain crimes, they called privilege, to their work positions, were forced to resign from their jobs, to reserve their dignities, and there were others who refused to resign. They were trial and convicted as criminals, using their work positions for personal reason, and ended up in prison.

Ulrica had her special task force set up surveillance cameras on some of the streets' light poles, around different areas of the inner city, where criminal activities were imminent in the ghettoes, her effort was to alleviate the crimes rate in these places, also places where youth gangs participate, selling drugs mainly rock cocaine in different areas of the communities, causing the users to become addicted, turning nice decent women and high school girls into street hookers, prostituting their bodies for the price of a rock, for just a hit, some of these women became a fifty cent bitch, under the addiction of this chemical substance, if that what it took for them to purchase a piece of crack cocaine.

This was a drug epidemic, once it was used by an individual, it was like a contagious disease, spreading rapidly among men and women, turning some of them into criminals, since men couldn't really prostitute their bodies, as successfully as woman can for sexual profit, they were robbing and stealing, and if they had to, they would kill for the thrill, this piece of drug gives them, and a moment later, they would be craving for another puff of this rock cocaine sensation, keeping them in a low inferior lifestyle of living or in and out of prison, until they decease.

Ulrica wandered why Negroes mainly occupied most cities ghettoes. Even people of mix ethnicity with black's blood as a part of their genetic system, dwelled in this ugly part of the city, now there are a few poor white people living there, waiting for the welfare system, to put them in a better position, after the downfall, life had caused them to witness, living the life of poor black and Hispanic people.

Ulrica found out that inner cities youth gangs violence were caused by drug dealers, under the control of corrupted politicians, and their crafty business constituencies, most of them were Caucasian people, conducting illegal business with people of South America, manufacturing such illegal drugs, and exporting them to the United States, utilizing black youths as their guinea pigs, extorting their positions in these neighborhoods, to profit from such illegal business real good.

Some of the black men in these communities were serving certain white men, as their hoodlums, utilizing these inner city's youths, as their drug pushing thugs. Ulrica had found out that these different youth gangs violent were organized and caused by these drug dealers, having these young black adolescences territorialize themselves as gang members, declaring war on each other as their drug selling competition increased, because one gang move off into another gang's territory selling drugs, causing a conflict, which ended as some gang members getting killed.

Ulrica had her task force apprehend all the gang members, she had seen on those surveillance cameras, clandestinely placed in different areas of these gang members' activities. They were brought together at Portland's basketball arena. Some of these gang members had lawyers there representing them. It was between the numbers of six to seven hundred of them. Some of their complexions were as light as day to as dark as night. The age of the youngest gang member was five, and the oldest one was twenty- seven.

Ulrica had those over the age of twenty arrested and charged with the crime of contributing to juvenile delinquency. She was walking among these young gangsters, with six of the biggest police officers, on her task force walking with her. She was speaking words of humiliation to their existences, not to intimidate them, but to make each feel guilty, for participating in such criminal activities. "I'm ashamed of you young men, most of you are black, degrading your own kind, who struggled over two hundred years or more, trying to gain the respect and appreciation of your race, many great black leaders lost their lives for equality. Now you young fools today, don't know or care about their effort, before you and what they went through, for your generation to be treated equal at least by the policemen."

Ulrica was getting angry by the thoughts of her being pregnant with a baby boy, and he too may ended up in such youth activities as these. She spoke bold and impudently. "You young black men have ashamed, the spirit of those black leaders, who have die for your freedom and civil right to live your lives as equal as other people, mainly Caucasian or white, the majority, and you are killing up each other, because you are ignorant to the face the fact, that certain people are using money and drugs, to turn you against one another, interfering with your future, most of you will end up dead or spending the rest of your lives, in and out of jail, and that is not a nice way to live your lives."

Ulrica continued her angry lecturing while walking through these young gang bangers, looking into their eyes without a smile, and they would drop their heads in shame, hearing what she's saying. "I'm asking you young men to stop using the 'N' word to insult one another. This is a racial insult, and it is against the law for a person of another ethnicity, to use it in the company of black people, and you, young punks use the word nigger, as simple as you are breathing, and you are disrespecting black women, by calling them whores and bitches, no other men of a different ethnicity treat their women like this."

Ulrica kept up her bluff. "Think about those who die, lost their lives, tying to change the rules of this society, so that you can be treated equal, and given the opportunity, to live a decent lifestyle, don't let their deaths be in vain." One of these thugs spoke out boldly. "What wrong with this whore, rounding us up like a bunch cattle, interrogating us without reading our rights first, shit, we young, but we are making good money, fuck that horny, nigger loving bitch."

Ulrica approached this guy, surrounded by these big policemen, plus she was carrying a gun herself under her arm. It wasn't seen, because she had her suit coat on. Ulrica starred this guy in his eyes. "The word whore is going to get you a bloody nose, and the words, niggers loving bitch, is going to get your stupid, booty switching ass kick." Ulrica threw a straight jab against this guy's face with enough force, knocking him to the floor with blood, running from his nose, then she kicked against his ass, while he lay there, holding his nose. Ulrica told her police officers. "Arrest this punk ass sissy for verbally assaulting the D.A." Two of the policemen snatched this guy up from the floor to his feet, and rushed him out of the arena to jail.

Ulrica began to speak insulting words to these gang members with tears of anger in her eyes. "Half of you have dropped out of schools, and you don't know what to do, some of you joined a group of drug pushing fools, trying to find your manhood. I have evident of the crimes, you have committed, all on video tapes, and some of you will be incarcerated, others will be placed on probation for such participation, don't you know crime doesn't pay, and it is my job to put criminals away, so you think this is cool, I bet half of you are confused faggots, trying to prove your manhood, a bunch of booties switching sissies."

Ulrica walked up to the biggest members of these gangs, and replied, "You don't like what I just said, what you want to do, you want to fight me." This thug quickly replied, "No, ma'am, Mrs. District Attorney." Ulrica replied out loud, "Those of you who will not be going to jail, I advise you to get your asses back in school, and leave those streets alone, stop selling drugs, because most of you are not grown, and those of you who are grown, your time have come, and I want you, young men to know what I'm trying to do, if a youth commits an adult crime, that youth will do an adult time."

Ulrica walked up to those five to twelve years old gang bangers replying, "I can have your parents arrested for the crimes you boys are committing, because they are neglecting their duties, as parents to see that you are properly reared as law abiding citizen, and I also know, there are certain white men, in charge of your gang leaders, who got you out there selling drugs, because of your age, jail is not the place, to discipline kids as young as you, don't be stupid out there, jeopardizing your young lives and freedom, trying to make these people richer, and when you get arrested, they get another young black guy to take your place."

Ulrica effort to disperse these growing gangs' activities worked, after she did, what she had threatened to do. She had all of their pictures taken and fingers printed. Whenever any of them were seen on those surveillance camera again, selling drugs or doing anything illegal, the policemen waited, until they went to the places, to lay their heads, and arrested them out of bed, into juvenile court with enough evident, to send them to criminal youth residents, jail or prison, taking them off the streets in numbers, causing the rest of them to stop their gang activities, enrolled back in schools, studying to live a more decent lifestyle. Ulrica was proud of such an accomplishment. Now she was at those criminals in the hierarch drugs dealing positions, if they got caught couldn't be proven guilty.

During Ulrica's pregnancy, she was very active the whole nine months, doing an impressive job as the District Attorney. She continued to do her calisthenics, prescribed for pregnant women. She and I would visit the shooting range together, enhancing our marksmanships, and she was an expert, when it came to shooting a pistol. We had licenses to carry concealed weapons, and a permit to kill, if it was necessary, in order to protect or prevent ourselves from getting killed. I would go to class with her, preparing to assist her, when she went into labor, to give birth to our baby.

Ulrica was successful with the use of her task force cleaning up the ghetto, arresting some of the main drugs dealers. A couple of clandestine informers were found dead. A police officer, who was on the take, was hired to kill them, and their friends were filled with enough remorse, to seek revenge. They retaliated by turning evident against this police officer, and he was arrested and trial for the crime he committed, and was sentenced life in prison.

Illegal drugs became so scant on the streets, until it was hurting the pockets, of some big time politicians in the business, of having illegal drugs imported into this state. Ulrica's task force have a shoot out with some ofthese drug people, during a rage at one of their main drugs facility, killing most of them, and the rest surrender, causing some of the affluent criminals, like certain bankers and politicians, alert the medias complaining about, the tactic being used by the D.A. task force.

Ulrica retaliated by investigating a few politicians, two well-known bankers, the owner of a television station, and a newspaper company for the suspicion of supporting illegal drug dealers, in the lower level of our community. Ulrica's task force had these drug dealers under control in the ghetto, so their business moved into the suburb, and Ulrica's task force attacked them there, with the support of the voters. Drug dealers were serving as ice cream vehicle drivers, delivering drugs and ice cream to different residents, who were ordering it, by a certain code numbers over the telephone, a couple of postmen were arrested for delivering illegal drugs with the mail.

Ulrica reputation as District Attorney was enhanced, and the citizen of her district, were supporting her with full promotion, to run for the United States Senator's seat in Washington, D.C. Ulrica said that she would have to give, the thought of being a law maker some serious considerations, before Ulrica knew it, her constituencies were campaigning for her to achieve the U.S. Senator's seat.

Ulrica and I had brought some land on the out skirt of town, and had a ranch style mansion built on it near the lake. it was big enough to accommodate friends, and family members when they come to visit. One night we were at home alone, somewhere during Ulrica's ninth month of pregnancy. She had taken maternity leave from work, waiting on her due date, filled with suspense, and I stop working on my written project, just to be there with her through such an experience.

Since this was such a big house, Ulrica and I slept upstairs in the bedroom. We would practice moving about the house at night in the dark, so that we would be familiar with it, just in case an unexpected situation occurred. Speaking of an unexpected situation, it happened the same night our house was burglarized. We were upstairs in the bedroom asleep. Ulrica heard something moving about downstairs in our kitchen. I was sound asleep, and she woke me. I thought she was having labor pain.

Ulrica whispered into my ear, "Bobby, darling, wake up, I hear something, moving around in our kitchen." I woke up, speaking, "What's wrong, are you in pain?" She replied, "No, be quiet, I think someone is downstairs, burglarizing our house, and it sound like, they are in the kitchen, get up and get your gun and the flash light, let's catch this stupid fool, in his criminal act." I quietly got out of bed, and got my 357 magnums, in one hand and the flashlight in my other hand. Ulrica had her 380 automatic pistols in her hand, walking behind me, and we slowly moved down the dark stairs into the kitchen.

We stood behind the wall of the kitchen and dining room, observing this tall heavyset person with a ski mask covering his face and head moving throughout the kitchen, taking all of our expensive kitchenware. He was putting them in a duffel bag, as he moved toward the open kitchen's window, I aimed the barrel of my gun at him, then I turned on the flash light, blinding his eye sight. I replied, "Halt, you are busted."

This hooded person started running toward the open window, and as he motioned the dive through the window, I fired a shot, hitting him in his buttock, knocking him into the kitchen window, breaking it. He hollered out loud from the pain of the bullet going through his butt, forcing his body to crash into the window. He dropped the duffel bag, breaking our crystal glass set, that we received as a wedding gift. When Ulrica heard that, she really got upset. She turned on the kitchen's light, cussing out loud at this burglar's body, hanging out of the broken window. "You stealing son-of-a-bitch, I ought to shot your roguish ass again, for breaking my got damn crystal set, come on baby, pull his ass back inside the house, because he's hanging too far out."

While I was pulling this burglar's body back inside the house, Ulrica was calling the police. This man was in pain. I let his body fall to the kitchen's floor. He was groaning and begging for some water, because his butt was burning from the bullet wound. I pulled the hood from his head.

This burglar appeared to be a male Caucasian. At the sight of his face, Ulrica's water broke, and she went into labor, falling to the kitchen's floor groaning out these words. "Oh, Bobby, this baby is coming for sure, oh, God, it's hurting, Bobby, please help me." I went to comfort my wife, while holding my gun on the burglar, ordering him to lay on his stomach with his hands behind his head.

When the police arrived, they searched the burglar, and found a gun in his pocket. Two ambulances arrived, one of the ambulance workers assisted Ulrica with her condition. The burglar was arrested, and taken to the hospital, by the other ambulance for his bullet wound, then to jail. I got into my car, and followed the ambulance with Ulrica in it to the hospital. Two police officers were told to stay and guard our house, until the window was repaired. At the hospital, the medical workers were rushing Ulrica into the delivery room. She was huffing and puffing from her pain, and I was nervous and worry, while getting dressed, to participate in the delivery of my baby. 1 became deliriously ambiguous, filled with the anxiety of seeing a production of me, until I had to calm myself mental, emotional and physically. I entered the delivery room with a calm and smooth attitude.

Ulrica was on the delivery table with her legs lifted and spread. I was glad her doctor was a female. I don't think I would appreciate, seeing a male doctor's hands, manipulating between my wife's legs like that. I went by Ulrica's side to encourage her to push harder, since she wanted to experience, giving natural birth to our first child, most of the delivering work as up to her. I began to coach her with these words. "Come on, baby, huff and puff, then push as hard as you can, it will be over within a minute." Ulrica looked at me with angry and painful tears, standing in her eyes replying, "Yeah, that is easy for you to say, just as easy as it was, for you to push yourself into me, causing all of this painful bullshit to happen, and nine months later, the more I see your face, the more piss off I get." I felt sort of insulted, after hearing her words, and I impudently replied, "Seem to me, you are not piss enough to shit this baby out."

Ulrica let out a prolong pissed off scream, after hearing those words coming from me. "Get away from me, I hate you, inconsiderable son-of-a- bitch, shheee! "She began to force the baby from her body, and the doctor called me, between her legs to catch my son's head, as he came into this world, crying out loud. I was so proud, until I almost pass out, from the nasty looking sight of him. I gently got a hold of him with the doctor help, before his feet were out of his mommy's body, he came into this world hollering out to life, crying.

Ulrica was overwhelmed with the release of giving birth to a seven and a half pound baby boy. The doctor had separated his naval cord, and the nurse took him to be cleaned up. They were congratulating us on our first borne son. I went to Ulrica, and kissed her exhausted lips, and she replied, "You know, I didn't mean those words, I said during that ordeal." I replied, "So didn't I, but it help out, I love my wife." She gave me a proud smile, and replied, "And I love my husband too, I really do."

The nurse came back into the delivery room with our son, cleaned and dressed, playing with him like he was hers, replying. "Oh, this is such a cute baby boy, Mr. and Mrs. Wilson, you two people should be proud, because you have produced one handsome baby boy, and he has such a cute little sexy smile." Ulrica replied, "Hurry, please, I will like to see the production of me." The nurse gave Ulrica our child, as she laid him into her arms. Ulrica looked at him, and he saw her, and began to smile. Ulrica replied, "Oh, he is so cute and lovely looking, a head full of curly black hair, with my colorful eyes, and he has your face's appearance, Bobby, darker than me, and he's lighter than you."

The baby started crying. The nurse replied, "He is ready for some food." Ulrica took out her breast, and began to feed him, looking at me replying, "Don't get jealous, these breasts are providing his meal, until I decided to put him on a milk bottle, and by the way, what are you going to name him." I replied, "Romance." Then she replied, "Let's name him, Bobby Romance Wilson, because he is a blessing from each of our genetic system, thank you, darling, for giving me such a lovely baby boy child, I love you so much, oh shit, he must be hungry, because he is really sucking hard on my breast, that hurts."

I walked up to Ulrica, while she was breastfeeding little Romance, and replied, "I love you for doing such a great job as my wife, giving birth to my first borne, and thank God, he's a healthy boy, our first son." Our lips met producing a gracious kiss. Ulrica's breast slip from little

Romance's mouth, and he let her know it, by crying out loud. I walked outside her hospital room, to talk to the doctor for a while, clandestinely requesting that she add a few extra stitches to my wife's vagina, so when that time comes again, it will fit more comfortably.

Three months later, Ulrica became a fanatic with her calisthenics. She was exercising her body with my coaching help, so that her body would become more sexually developed, her complexion was glowingly smooth again, because during her pregnancy and afterward, she continually used co- co butter, until there was no stress marks, showing on her body from giving child birth. We both participated in parenting little Romance, together we would bath him, and at night during his crying spell, we would take turn, walking the floor with him in our arms, singing songs while rocking him, until he falls asleep, releasing us of a sleepless night.

Ulrica returned to work with a different hairstyle, shorter in length with a more intellectual sex appeal for a lady in such a dominating position. Although she continued her work as district attorney, Ulrica was focusing on being elected to the seat of the United States senator, that when the surprise of her life arrived in her office. Ulrica had an illegitimate brother by her father and a black woman without anyone in her family knowing about him.

Ulrica had just finished a conference with her assistant D.A. telling them what fine jobs they were doing. She praised their expertise, and they gave her their support for her run for the U.S. senator's seat. As they left the conference room, a light complexioned black man with a face feature similar to hers approached Ulrica. He spoke to her with words of congratulation. "Hell, Mrs. D.A. Wilson, my name is Johnny Smith, the sub-name belong to my mother, since you are married to a black man with a biracial child. I thought you wouldn't be reluctant to accept me as your half-brother."

Ulrica starred at this man with agape lips. She sort of hesitated with her reply. "Ah, who, when, where, or how, never mind all of that, come into my office and let me regroup, and get better acquainted with you." Johnny replied, "How about lunch together, I'm a medical doctor. We have the same father, daddy Frank never wanted me to know about his legitimate family, because of his infidelity with my mother, but he took good care of us. He made sure gangs didn't trap me, and he inspired me to go to college, and study to be a doctor. He also paid for my education, since you are married to a black man, I thought it would be candid of me to reveal my identity to you, and I hope, you allow me to see my little nephew, before I leave this country, to continue my career as a medical doctor in Africa, because they need my expertise the most. I'm determined to do something good for that side of my ethnicity."

Ulrica and Johnny were seen having lunch together by some of my friends, and they misunderstood their togetherness. I was receiving telephone calls, telling me, my wife is been seen having lunch with a color man. Ulrica invited Johnny to our house to meet little Romance and me. Everything was lovely for us to share some moments of our lives with him, before he goes to Africa. Johnny was married to an African princess, named Natasha, from the country Algeria. She was a tall lady with smooth dark coffee brown complexion, intellectually attractive.

She met Johnny in college while she was serving as an exchanged student at the University of Washington. She majored in Physics, a straight "A" student with her minor study Political Science, with the interest of returning to her homeland, inspiring the leaders of her country to take more interest in modern technology, to be in the top running up position, of being one of the most powerful countries on earth.

Ulrica invited Natasha to a meeting, held by a club of women known as the Intellectual Ladies Organization, in which Ulrica was their chairperson. At the meeting, Ulrica amazed her members by introducing Natasha to them as her sister-in-law, the wife of her surprisingly half-brother, who she just met. Natasha gave a speech to the members of this club on the inspiration of successful women. She emphasized the importance of individuality over ethnicity.

Johnny and I did a few things together as brothers-in-laws. We went to a sport bar, had a couple of drinks, and shot a game or two of billiard. Ulrica gave up her ticket to this pro football game, I had for her to Johnny, so he and I went to see the Seahawk play to Cowboys at the Seahawk's stadium that Sunday's afternoon, before that, we watched a televised championship fight that Saturday night, while Ulrica and Natasha did ladies things together.

Johnny and I talked about the political interest of Algeria's professional athletes, and what it would take for them to enhance their sport playing abilities to be in the competition with the best of American and European's professional athletes. They have recruited different professional people in the field of technology, agricultural science, medicine, business enhancement, and military strategy.

Natasha, Ulrica, Johnny and I spent three days together with little Romance having dinner, and going to different activities with a family like setting. Then we hired ourselves a baby sitter for little Romance, while the four of us visited our favorite nightclub. I danced with Natasha, while Ulrica danced with her half-brother. They were trying to get better acquainted with each other. Whenever Johnny challenged me in a game of pool, tennis, or domino, a one on one competition, Ulrica would be pulling for her brother to win, just to make him feel good, and Natasha was pulling for me to win, because she admired my manhood, as a successful writer and an inspiration to my wife.

We heard a brief history of Johnny's existence. He was two years younger than Ulrica. His mother was a young black female dancer, who was hired by Frank D'Angelo, the owner of the nightclub, where she applied as a dancer. Her name was Nicole, an attractive black single lady, and Frank clandestinely began to date her on several occasions, and he fell in love with her, and began to pay her to be his mistress. She got pregnant. Frank refuse to let her have an abortion, and took on the responsibility as Johnny illegitimate father, and made sure Johnny grew up in a nice environment, receiving the proper education to be intellectually successful.

Although Ulrica held a grudge against her father, she never did talked about his infidelity, against her mother all of those years Johnny didn't exist. Now a year later, Frank D'Angelo, his brother Stanley, her two brothers Sumner and Silas, also Taylor and Terence, Ulrica first cousins, the sons of her uncle Stanley. They came to our house, acting all nice and friendly, playing with Romance, then they invited me out for dinner, that when Ulrica interrupted them replying, "Wherever my husband goes with you, I'm going too, for security reason, because I don't trust him alone with none of you, and that's the truth."

They invited Ulrica out for dinner with us, and she told Marcie, our Mexican nanny, a young attractive lady to take Romance into his room, and prepare him for bed. She then whispered into my ear, "Arm yourself, I have a feeling tonight, I'm have to arrest my family members." Ulrica and I drove our car following the three cars; they were in, to their place of business, a nice looking nightclub with a casino.

We were invited to a special room with a bar, pool table, conference table with chairs. Frank ordered up some food for us to eat. We have a few drinks, and Frank asked me to shoot a game of pool with him, while he discussed a business proposition with me.

Ulrica had excused herself from our presence, and went into the lady's room with her cellar phone in her purse. She called up her special task force, and prepared them to rage this place of business, whenever she gave them the words to do so. While Frank and I were shooting pool, we were tied a two game apiece, his brother, two sons, and nephews were standing around listening and encouraging me to accept his offer in becoming a partner of his illegal money making business under legal pretension.

Frank was speaking to impress me. "Now Bobby, I admitted. I was sort of piss off about you dating my Ulrica, but after you two got married, and now I have a grandson by you two, we all family now, and this is my way of accepting you as my son-in-law. I would like for you to become a partner of this family, owning and operating a four stories building, on the out skirt of the suburb, where there will be more money spent on buying our drugs, and enjoying the company of people of different ethnicities as customers and employees of this four into one business featuring a night club, restaurant, casino, and motel."

I replied, "I don't know. Ulrica will be totally against, my involvement in this type of business." Frank replied, "Ah, horse shit, she won't resist the idea, if you insist on being a partner of this business, you see we are leaving the ghetto alone, because Ulrica's drug task force there are too strong. They have confiscated nearly a billion dollar's worth of drugs from our warehouses and the streets, plus they have incarcerated some of our best connections.

"Now we are focusing on intelligent moneymaking people, and we would like for you to recruit some of your influential friends to be your partner in dealing with the black people. There will be an espresso shop set up throughout the city, doing undercover drugs dealing, see, Bobby Wilson, we can be billionaires with this type of business."

I only shook my head, indicating no. Frank replied, "What you mean about that?" Ulrica entered the room replying impudently, "He means hell no! You spaghetti eating, cheating ass son-of-a-bitch. Why in the fuck, you are trying to get my husband into this type of trouble? He is not going to participate in your got-damn illegal business. Why not your illegitimate son, Johnny, oh you thought I wouldn't have found out about him, hah daddy Frank."

Ulrica two brothers and cousins started walking toward Ulrica replying, "Cool it, sis, you are talking too much shit, to papa here." Ulrica spoke out bold to them. "You pizza eating chumps, your best is to back out of this dispute, because this mother fucker, been cheating on my mother with women of other ethnicities, while teaching his children, at home with him to be prejudice toward black and other minority people, so that lie can keep his secret of using these women as his mistress. Are there any more bastard around, related to us?"

Frank replied in Italian mixed with English. "Yes, there is, and she is mixed with Chinese, I met her mother in San Diego. Don't you forget who your father is, I'm the one who cause you to be here, and if you keep disrespecting me, I'm being the one who will cause you to decease?

"Now I don't know what kind of penis or tongue this Negro is using on you, but you better take notice who the fuck, you are talking to, once again I'm you father-got-damn it, I brought you into this world, and I will take your nigger loving ass out, just as fast, you don't sass me, I'm your dad."

Ulrica became infuriated with Frank replying, "If you can't comprehend my articulation, I suggest that you get yourself an interpreter, if you want to farther this conversation between us, because it seems, as though, you are having problems with my vocabulary, and if you were more educated, you will understand what I'm saying, intellectually speaking, you need to read my lips, because I have made my decision. You are guilty for the crimes, you have committed, and you will be sentenced to prison for threatening me, I'm a public official, you are under arrest mister D'Angelo."

Mr. D'Angelo spoke out boldly. "Just because you are married to this negro, no smart ass daughter of mine is going to talk to me like this." Ulrica let out a scream. "Bobby, pull your weapon." She went into an ass-kicking fix. She began to maneuver her body with such physical agility among her brothers and cousins, who were trying to prevent Ulrica, from attacking her father with her fists and feet, plus some judo technique.

Ulrica was sending each of them falling to the floor, groaning while holding their crotches and faces. She fought her way throughout her brothers and cousins, defeating them physically. I had pulled my weapon from my shoulder's holster under my coat, ready to shoot any and everyone, who was about to pull a gun. Ulrica's uncle Stanley stepped in front of her, and before he could speak, she attacked him physically, sending him colliding to the floor with a bloody nose.

By that time, the task force was kicking the door down, shouting out with laser beams guns pointing at everyone, all right everybody get down on the floor. Frank threw a hard punch at his daughter, as though she was a man, and Ulrica evaded getting hit by his fist, and she retaliated by punching hard against his face. Some of her task force members grabbed a hold of Frank, so he couldn't defend himself, and Ulrica took her frustration out on her father, until he passed out. She punched him unconscious, and then she ordered her task force to arrest the rest of her relatives, and charged them with the conspiracy of trying to bribe her husband into racketeer.

This incident made the newspaper's headline. District Attorney with the aid of her task force arrested the city main drug king, her father Mr. Frank D'Angelo and five of her relatives. Frank, his brother, two sons, and two nephews were released from jail by bail, and they exile from the United States back to Italy. Ulrica put a twenty five thousand dollars bounty out for anyone who assists in having each of them arrested. Later, Ulrica received a telephone call from her mother, and they had a heated conversation in Spanish.

Now Ulrica was campaigning for the U.S. Senator's seat, she was interested in having certain laws changed. She thought criminalizes only minority people, mainly those with dark complexions or African descent was illegal. She also wanted to add some laws pertaining to the legalization of certain drugs, making it illegal for business people to overcharge their customers for certain products sub charges and illegal fee, also laws pertaining to social activities, and fair employment laws to be strictly enforced.

Ulrica was campaigning diligently to convince enough constituencies to put her in the U.S. Senator's seat, and during an outdoor concert in the city's park, we were there enjoying the entertainment. Our main purpose for being there was to inspire more people to vote.

When we decided to leave, we were confronted by trouble, while Ulrica and I were walking from the outdoor concert toward our car. We were armed with our concealed weapons, and were wearing a bulletproof vest each, because of the arresting conflict Ulrica encountered, with her father and other family members. I was afraid, someone would try to assassinate us, because Frank D'Angelo was a powerful drug king in that region of the country.

Before we could get to our car in the parking lot, a tall healthy built black man came toward us, looking like a pro football player. He stood about six feet, seven or eight inches tall, weighing about three hundred and fifty pounds. He approached us in a derogatory manner replying impudently. "Say pimp, how much you want for this bitch here." Ulrica was insulted, and I was humiliated by his rudeness, and Ulrica was ready to fight replying with street sense. "A bitch is a female dog, if you are in heat, go and fuck your mother, because she is more like a bitch than me." This big dude replied, "Ah, you nigger loving whore, I'm about to fuck you and your husband."

That when I lit into his face with my fists, throwing a velocity of punches, flooding his face with the knuckles of my combination of jabs.

He was staggering and stumbling, but he didn't fall. I was punching him hard and talking noise. "You big black stupid, booty switching, asshole licking, punk ass motherfucking nigger, somebody push you up to this. Why you want to come fucking with us, I'm beat your got-damn ass, until you shit on yourself. This is my wife, motherfucker! You got five seconds to apologize." I was maneuvering around him with such physical agility, causing him to miss, each time he threw a punch at me.

This big man took all of my punches, before he grabbed me, into a bear hug, lifting me up off of my feet. He was about to body slam to the ground. That when Ulrica attacked him with a stiff kick against his crotch. He folded over, trying not to drop me, and then Ulrica gave him a painful kick, against the side of his ankle and knee. He let out a loud holler, before falling to the ground, still holding on to me. He landed on top of me, I was lying on my back, fighting him like a cat, punching against his face and head, while he held me there.

He was struggling hard, groaning out his pain, trying to punch down against my face, that when Ulrica tore the heel off of her shoe, kicking against the side of his face and head, blood splattered from his face. He grabbed a hold of his face, while rolling away from me. That when Ulrica and I began to beat him mercifully, people began to gather around us, replying, "Oh, they are tearing his ass up, that what that big motherfucker get for starting trouble." The police arrived on the scene.

I thought, that I would have to pull out my gun, because some of the spectators were getting close, instigating that we were trying to kill this guy, replying, "Ah, man, look how they are beating on home boy, I don't like this shit, one bit." When the police arrived, everybody stepped aside. This man was arrested for assaulting the District Attorney and her husband, but the consequence was detrimental to his physical condition, and he swore that we attacked him, and he was incarcerated for assaulting a public official.

Ulrica was campaigning hard to be elected to the U.S. Senator's seat. She was facing stiff competition, challenging her interracial marriage. There was this Caucasian anthropologist with a serious ethnocentric attitude, claiming that Ulrica was ethnically insane, because she was married to a black man. His philosophy on mixing ethnicities went like this. It is acceptable for people of different nationalities, to intercourse with each other intimately, just as long as they are people of different gender, but when it come to indulging with people of different ethnicities, this creates a social disease called mixed ethnicities, taking the purity out of certain race of people.

Dr. Fuross was this anthropologist name. He was an intellectual racist, who wrote a book titled: "Keeping Your Ethnicity Pure." He expressed his prejudice on seeing people of different ethnicities producing children together, just to make them look physically better, but this can be a curse against their mentalities, spreading the thought that the white European Caucasian people are losing the purity of their superiority, by mixing their blood with people of lower or inferior ethnicities, such as Asian and African descent. Dr. Fuross claimed by mixing people of different ethnicities were like breeding different animals to create another kind of animal.

This approach by Dr. Fuross was a threat to the people of this nation who believe in true democracy. Ulrica spoke on enhancing the civil right law for all American citizen, to be treated with equality, described in the concept of the moderate creed throughout this country's existence, initiated by the thirty fifth president of the United States, I was in the sixth grade, living the life of segregation, down south of the U.S.A. It was one hot summer day, during the month of August; President Kennedy had addressed the Nation with his speech. He was answering questions from news reporters. "Mr. President, do you think the Negro people should have as much right as white people?" He made his usual remark with humor, smiling with his head down, then he raised his head, looking seriously into the television cameras, then he said, "Yes, I think the Negro people should have just as much right as the white, and as a matter of fact, it will become a law today as I speak." He initiated integration for this nation that day, and three months later, he was assassinated, causing the world great frustration, because he did what was right for the human race.

The year was two thousand and six, Ulrica campaign strategy prevailed her with victory over her adversary, and she was asked would being a wife and a mother interfere with her job, representing her constituency as a United States Senator. Ulrica spoke convincingly. "No, I as a working wife and mother can take home the bacon and cook it too, also I will have enough time to sit down, and eat it with my family too, because raising a family won't interfere with my political obligation. My job as senator is to represent my constituency, listen to what they have to say, whether it complaints, advices, comments or suggestions on what should be written as the law or deleted. My job is to serve my constituency truly, and I'm still capable of being a loving wife to my husband and a caring and emotional concern mother for my son."

When Ulrica gave birth to our first child, Bobby Romance, we nick named him Bobby J. We were given a Great Dane's puppy as a gift to grow up with him. We named this dog, Troy, and a year later; he had grown into the size of a pony. He was a tall, large, powerful dog. He would pull Bobby J. around in his wagon, and Bobby J. would ride on his back.

Whenever Troy would hear Bobby J. crying, he would come to see what was wrong with him. Although Ulrica was a respectful politician, we still enjoyed life together as family members, continue doing our bodies developing exercises, playing different types of game together, jogging and bike riding, I mostly be running while pushing Bobby J. in his stroller.

One day Ulrica, Bobby J., Troy and I were having an evening walk through the inner part of the city, slowly but surely drug dealers were working their way back into that area of the Portland. I was pushing the stroller with Bobby J. in it, and Ulrica was walking beside me with Troy on a leash ahead of her. We were having a nice conversation, when a foolish drug addict ran by us, and snatched Ulrica's purse. She didn't try to resist him. She practically gave the purse to him. This seems to be Hispanic or biracial man, and he was running away fast. Ulrica shouted out, "Stop, thief, bring my purse hack, before I sic my dog on your ass."

This guy kept running, and Ulrica released Troy from his leash replying, "Sic him, boy, go and get him." Troy began to bark while chasing this guy. He ran the guy down, tackling him to the ground, biting and slinging him around. The guy was hollering out loud from the pain Troy was putting on him with his teeth. "Oh, please, call your dog off of me, he is killing me." We took our time pulling Troy away from this man's bit up body. Troy did some serious damage to his arms, legs and the side of his body. This man protected his face and neck with his hands and arms, trying to keep Troy away from him.

The police arrived and called an ambulance to the scene. This man was hospitalized for his dog bite wounds. After he was released from the hospital, he spent some time in jail for snatching Ulrica's purse.

Ulrica was working as an U.S. senator, going back and forward to Washington, D.C. representing her constituency as a member of the nation's legislative bodies, making laws and discussing problems. Ulrica wanted this country to focus more on its domestic problems, and she was suggesting certain laws being proposed, be written and passed in the interest of the common or less fortunate citizen.

Bobby J. was two years old, learning how to talk and doing other things, a child at that stage of life will normally do. I enjoyed taking him to the park with me, because he seemed to have eyes for beautiful women, and on different occasions, he has walked up to an attractive lady, speaking to her, telling her his name, and asking her name. She would talk to him complimentingly as being a cute, handsome and smart little boy. Bobby J. would take her by the hand, and lead her to the bench where I be sitting replying to her, "Come say hi to dad-dad, say hi to her dad." Each lady and I would introduce ourselves to each other, and end up holding a decent conversation about child rearing. I believe, if I hadn't mentioned that I was the husband of congresswoman D'Angelo-Wilson, some of these ladies would have shown more intimate interest in me.

One day Ulrica and I were talking about how Bobby J. was growing, and she told me about the day she took Bobby J. walking through the park, and he led her to a man, the way he led women to me. I got jealous and called Bobby J. a little traitor. I told Ulrica about the women, he led to me at the park. Ulrica only laugh, replying, "He's only trying to be friendly, but you keep an eye on him around strange people, this is a habit, we need to stop him from doing, because if someone kidnap my son, oh God, I think, I will die, after I kill you first for letting it happen. It's time to be more secure and teach him not to be friendly with strangers." I replied in a joking way, "His friendly attitude caused me a few girlfriends." Ulrica responded, "I met a few boyfriends too, but this is the end of him being friendly, until he gets older."

I couldn't wait, until Bobby J. becomes the age and size for me to teach him how to box, play football, baseball, basketball, tennis, golf and other sports. One day I had him in the back yard playing with a football, something I would usually do, and sometime Ulrica would join in, running the football, and I would slowly her tackle to the ground with Bobby J. falling on top of us. This particular day, I was running around Bobby J. faking him to the ground. Each time he fell to the ground, he would get angry, so I tossed the ball nice and slow for him to catch it, and he ran up to the ball with his hands open too wide, and caught the ball with his face, the ball hit against his nose. His nose started bleeding, and he ran into the house hollering and screaming.

Ulrica got upset with me, and began to nag at me about playing with him to rough. I made it worse by telling her not to interfere with my son disagreement with me. Those words turned our dispute into an altercation. Ulrica asked Marcie to take Bobby J. into his room, and give him a bath, before she went off on me speaking bodaciously. "I dare you to tell me some bullshit tike that, I was the one who nourished him for nine months, and went through all those pain, birthing him into this world. He is my son more than yours, and I mean got damn it, don't be playing rough with him like that again."

Ulrica accusation pissed me off, and I replied, "Look, woman, you better cool your attitude, just because you are Mrs. Politician of the year, I'm not your constituencies, and you are not convincing for me to hear, I'm the man of this house, and your husband, and don't you talk to me that way again, because you are not going to kick my ass, like you did your daddy, brothers and cousins." Ulrica became more aggressive;

she stood in her self-defense stand. I replied, "Don't let the consequent of your action be detrimental to your emotional existence. She replied with gritting teeth. "Leave, Bobby, just get away from me, before I do something, later I will regret."

I rushed out of the house, ran to my car, got into it quick, and drove away fast. It was night when I returned home. I had gotten myself too intoxicated to drive home. A friend of my drove me home, and I entered the house staggeringly drunk, went through the bedroom, on into the bathroom. Ulrica had taken a shower, sitting on the bed, lotioning her body, preparing to go to a banquet held by the women league honoring her success.

When I staggered out of the bathroom into the master bedroom where Ulrica was dressing herself, she looked at me in a concern way replying, "Bobby, darling, are you alright? I'm sorry about today." I turned around and walked back into the bathroom replying, "Yeah, you are forgiven, I need to take a shower." After I took a cold shower, I was somewhat sober, drying my body off with a large towel, walking into the bedroom with the towel wrapped around the waist of my body, going to the bedroom's dresser's draw to get a pair of my brief.

I was putting my brief on, when I looked toward Ulrica, sitting in front of her make-up dresser, dressed in her thong and bra, fixing up her face and hair, smelling stimulatingly fresh and sweet as she replied to me, "I did mention to you about the banquet, being given by the women league, honoring me tonight. You must have forgotten, after our fight." I replied in a drunken voice, "I haven't forgotten how horny, I get, after seeing you dress like that." I walked to her, and began to caress my hand against the smooth soft flesh of her back, while kissing soft wet words into her ear. "I'm requesting to see your beautiful breasts."

Ulrica was ovulating, and my foreplay technique began to stimulate her sexual interest. She replied, "Bobby, darling, can this wait, until after the banquet, because it is a special celebration for me." I replied, "Have you forgotten, being married to me is special too, you are neglecting your obligation to me as my wife. We haven't made love nearly two weeks. I know you monthly cycle doesn't last that long. Is there's another man, and you want me to move on?"

Ulrica turned to face me replying, "Now you are talking non sense, there is no other man of my concern, but your son, and I'm sorry, you feel as though, I'm neglecting you, oh, Bobby, you are making me feel so good, I don't know what to do." I lead Ulrica to the bed, reclining her body on it, as I removed her bra, and began to devour a sucking technique on her erected nipples, then the telephone began to ring. Ulrica answered it, and it was Joan, the chairperson of the women league. Ulrica replied to her in a moaning voice. "Oh, Joan, may I ask you a special favor, will you please accept my award, and lie for me.

"You see, I came down with this fever, and he got me burning up with lust. I have neglected my husband too long, and I'm obligated to let him play with me in an intimate way, before he finds another lady, then I really be frustrated. It been two weeks, and we are full of heat." Joan started laughing, before she replied, "Sound like, you are in too deep to quit anyway, don't worry, 1 will take your place, go ahead and make another baby."

And that exactly what we did, stay in our bedroom for two days, sexually romancing each other, as though we were long lost lovers, who have just found each other, playing different sexual games to entertain ourselves, even Marcie thought that we were sick. She came knocking at our bedroom's door that morning, after Ulrica and I had just finished making each other feel like paradise. Marcie replied after she knocked, "Oh, I'm sorry, but if you'll decent, Bobby J. want to come in, and play with you'll for a while."

Ulrica replied, "Wait a minute, Marcie, come on, Bobby, let's put on our pajamas, so Bobby J. can come in and play, without seeing his mother and father with no clothes on." We got dressed in our pajamas. Ulrica replied, "Okay, Marcie, Bobby J. can come in now." Marcie opened the door to our bedroom, and Bobby J. came running into it, jumping into the bed with us. I started tap boxing with him, and Ulrica pulled him away from me replying, "Come to mama, baby, before you get punched in the nose."

Ulrica cuddled Bobby J. into her arms, as he got under the bed cover, he replied, "Oh, mama, I feel something wet on my foot." Ulrica replied quickly, "Oh, yes, daddy had an accident, you see he been sick, that is why, we been in here most of the time, I'm trying to make him well again." Bobby J. looked at me and replied, "Will you discipline daddy for his accident, like you and Marcie disciplined me, when I use to accident in my bed?" I replied, "Mama was the one who caused me to have such an accident." Ulrica replied, "That is not true, daddy is just playing with you, have you eaten your breakfast yet, give mama a hug and a kiss, and go and fed yourself, until we get out of bed, then daddy, you and I are going to spend the rest of this day together, doing whatever you want to do, because daddy feel better already."

Each time we make love like that all day in bed, doing it long and sort of rough, a month later pregnancy is the result. Here how Ulrica tells me the good news. "Now I hope you are satisfied, because we are about to have another child." I replied, "Good, and I hope it be a girl, just as pretty as her mother." Ulrica came to me with kissing lips replying, "If she's going to look as good as her mother, we better go into the bedroom, and make sure she's fully bloomed."

During Ulrica nine months of pregnancy, every now and then, she would show an outrageous attitude toward me, claiming because of her pregnancy, I don't look at her with stimulating eyes anymore, and when we make love, it only occurred, because she requested for me to add zest to our sex. On the contrary to her accusation of me neglecting her, because she felt unattractive to me being pregnant. We had sex more often during her second pregnancy then her first.

I pampered her more during this pregnancy, buying her different gifts, taking her out for dinner, concepts, movies, and different theater performances, trying to impress her emotional interest of being her husband, showing her all of my loving. Each time she got a chance to get away from working as a U.S. senator, she and I would get together for a night out of town to a romantic resort.

I was working on a written project titled: "Being Married to a Female Politician." Ulrica's action to be a respectful and admirable woman working in the field of her profession, inspired me to write a book like this, but her loneliness for me as her husband became an addiction to her. She acted as though she couldn't get enough of us making love. This went on into her ninth month of pregnancy; I thought she might go into labor while we were indulging into such pleasure, because her sounds of pleasure would get loud and scary.

Ulrica didn't give birth to our second child, until I was away from home on the road, promoting this book, she advised me to write, showing love and care for her constituency, like a mother rearing her children to be successful citizens. She wanted the civil right laws enhanced, a law against homeless people be protected by the constitution. She thought this nation should always be obligated to feed its hungry citizens. She wanted to defeat racism, lower the crime rate, and give policemen and teachers pay raises with higher work prestige.

Ulrica had a meeting with thirteen of this nation most affluent and influential people to discuss her issue on true democracy. She wanted to run for president of the United States under a third party known as The Moderate Party. A political party that is affiliated with domestic concern with the welfare of this country's human right, employees and employers relation, wages, equality and the respect and dignity of each individual citizen.

These thirteen elite of the United States listened to what Ulrica had to say, and they were impressed by her intelligence and concern for the people of this country living out the true creed of democracy. They advised her to run for the governor's seat of the state of Oregon, and present her ideas to the people of that state. If she wins, and become a successful governor. She will be nominated to run for the president of the United States with their suppose.

Ulrica was so elated from the meeting, she had with these thirteen U.S. elites, until on her way from this meeting, she went into labor, her water broke while she was driving home with Marcie and Bobby J. in the car with her. Marcie was there to assist Ulrica, and took over the steeling wheel, drove Ulrica to the hospital, where she gave birth to a baby girl. Mrs. D'Angelo, Ulrica's mother arrived at the hospital in a hurry, as soon as she heard about Ulrica going labor, while they were in the car, driving to the hospital, talking to Mrs. D'Angelo on a cellar phone.

Mrs. D'Angelo suggested that Ulrica names her first daughter Victoria Valentine Wilson. Vee-Vee was her nickname. She had Ulrica's face appearance, with light honey brown eyes and bright bluish green center and trimming. She was a bit darker than Bobby J. complexion. Vee-Vee was a cute little girl. Her beautiful eyes would always sparkle, whenever she smile, and she would get happy, whenever she see me. I called her Baby-Girl.

Bobby J. was a bit jealous of Vee-Vee. He asked Ulrica where did she come from, and Ulrica reply honestly, "Bobby J., this is your sister, she came from me. I went to the hospital to have her deliver from my stomach, you remember that day, mama got sick in the car, and Marcie drove me to the hospital. You were in the car with us." Bobby J. replied, "I don't like her, take her back to the hospital, I don't want a baby sister." Ulrica took her time convincing Bobby J. to accept Vee-Vee as a new family member, his sister.

After Marcie or Ulrica bath Vee-Vee and put baby oil and powder on her body, dressing her. Vee-Vee would be looking and smelling like a cute little angel, and I enjoyed holding and playing with her that way, until we both would fall asleep, sitting in my personal chair with her in my arms. Ulrica or Marcie would come and take Vee-Vee from my sleeping arms, and put her in her bassinet or crib. Bobby J. was jealous of Vee-Vee and me. He became friendlier toward me, and Ulrica would show him favoritism as her way of showing her jealousy toward Vee-Vee and me, father and daughter relationship.

Vee-Vee was eighteen months old, when Ulrica position with the U.S. senator was about to expire, instead of running for re-election. Ulrica made an audacious move under the influence of her sponsors and political friends, also members of this unique women club she belonged to. It was during the year two thousand and eight, when Ulrica began to campaign for the state of Oregon's governor's seat, and the issue of her campaign became very heated. Ulrica's campaign strategy was against racism, illiteracy, domestic crimes and violence, and to enhance big businesses and the community relations, consumer affairs, employees and employers issues, humane concern, a cleaner environment, homeless and hungry citizen, free medical assistant for all citizen, and she lectured throughout her campaign that it would take an consummative integrated lifestyle to live out the true meaning of democracy.

Ulrica and members of her Moderate political party moved throughout the state of Oregon, inspiring people of different political parties to become her constituency, and help her win the state governor's seat, because the future demands an innovated political existence, and it can began in the state of Oregon, a territory that was discovered by a black man.

I went on some of those campaign trips with Ulrica, and her political followers. Some of the places, we took our son and daughter, with their nanny Marcie of course. Ulrica wanted a job, where she can execute equality, and I was reluctant to interfere with her dream, knowing that it would be difficult for her to succeed, married to me, a man of the dark complexion ethnicity, but to prove my love for her, I compromised with her decision, after negotiating through a strong debate, and she argued her point, until I was convinced, that in such a position as this, she could enhance the interracial relationship throughout this state.

With my support, Ulrica felt confident in her ability to win the governor's seat. She campaigned in different ethnical communities such as: African- American, Asian American, European-American better known as Caucasian or White American, also Hispanic and Native-American, people of other non- black or white ethnicities.

Ulrica was gaining the majority of these communities support for the change in humanity, and her campaign strategy was challenged by a group of people from each community, and she won their confident with intellectual wisdom by utilizing the skill of savoir-faire, proving to me that knowledge is power, and the ability to use such knowledge convincingly is wisdom.

She visited different level of schools: elementary, junior and high school, discussing with the students their future intensions, and the roles they would have to play as decision making people.

Ulrica had to face her opposition on racism. While discussing the subject of racism, Ulrica was confronted by ex and present members of white militant hate groups such as Klansmen, Nazism and other organization against integration, mostly Caucasian men, expressing their hatred or depreciation toward the existence of people, other than Caucasian mingling with white women. These men claimed, that Ulrica was trying to devalue the white race, by alleviating their ethnocentric attitudes. They also claimed that the United States is a white man's country, and white men, from the beginning until the end, will rule it.

Ulrica's response was that people occupied this country, when the European invaded it, and if this country belong to any ethnicity, it belong to its native citizens the American Indian. Another man spoke out loud. "Lady, why are you conspiring against us good folks, for the existence of those lazy no good, conniving and thieving ass niggers, spies, chinks, savages and all those other ass holes, coming into this country from the world over, we call minority, trying to steal citizenship, because they are inferior to the existence of American white people.

Ulrica replied, "History tells us that this country's grace as a great nation was contributed by migrants from different nations around the world. People of different nationalities, representing their ethnicities worked this country, with their sweat and blood. Some gave their lives in order for this country to survive different aggressions, and I just don't understand, why certain Caucasian people possess so much prejudice, toward the black citizen.

"Who have more right to be prejudice toward the white race, for forcing their ancestors into this country as slaves, and those racial words, that you used, only showed that you are, a stupid ass nincompoop, with a racial attitude, and if I'm elected as governor of this state, there will be a law against such expression, racial name calling will be a crime, penalty will be a fine and jail time.

"We can't re-live the life of yesterday, but tomorrow can bring a better way, to live for all citizen of the United States, if we can only collaborate, with each other, in a compromising way."

Another Caucasian man spoke out his stupidity, because he was reared as an ignorant human being. "Now let me make sense here, I learned to hate black people, because my grandparents taught my parents to hate them, because they were considered back then, as being less than human beings.

They were inferior to white people, because God was told to be the color of clear water or light, and the color white is closer to the color of water or light than black. They were illiterate back then, most of them couldn't read or write, and most of us white folks didn't know what the hell, they were talking about, mumbling out their words, while looking down at the ground.

They couldn't be understood, and the reason why they were called niggers, because they were illiterate, conniving and sneaky. Some of those fool ass black men would rape white women, because back then white women to them were like having sex with heaven, and they would end up meeting death."

Ulrica replied with an angry voice, "Mister, you have been badly misinformed, back then as you said, slaves weren't allow to read or write, nor were they allowed to look at white people while talking to them.

Black people have been mistreated in this country, and I'm talking about wrongly done, more than any other non white ethnicity, and it is not about the color of the skin, that makes a person a superb human being, nor the ethnicity of his or her kind, it all about the quality of that individual's mind with his or her ability to utilize it as a mean of competition.

If given an equal chance, to learn what is being taught, it has been proven, that black people with quality education, are intelligent people, especial when they are treated with equality. Superiority has nothing to do with the color of your skin, you should know that by now, there are more and more black people entering into dominating positions, that were once occupied only by white people, equality is a blessing to all ethnicities, and may the best person wins, without being judged by the color or his or her skin."

Ulrica paused for a moment, before speaking out these words. "Black people have made some great contributions to this country, and it has been hidden from the U.S. history books from the beginning, when this country fought Great Britain for its independent, and it was a black man by the name of Ethan Allen who instigated the American Revolution against the British soldiers, and he was the first to die for such a cause.

"There were other black men who fought in that war to make this country a free nation, to do what they wanted, and not what the British said, and what happen to the black people of this country, during George Washington, the first president of the United States administration, black people were forced into slavery, mainly by the southern states, and it took some two hundred odd years later, during the administration of the sixteenth president Abraham Lincoln, when the black people were freed, from such in-humane treatment, and this president was assassinated while sitting in a theater.

"His job wasn't finished. It took the 35th president, John F. Kennedy to execute a law, that gave black citizen of this country, equal right just as the white, and every war the United States fought in, there were black men there, fighting and losing their lives, as a part of the U.S. military, and I can't understand why so many white people, are racially prejudice against the black citizen of this country. Is it because in general, white people are jealous of the fact, that if black people on an individual base are given an equal chance, he or she will prove to be a better woman or man."

Another man spoke out loud. "Hell naught, that ain't what it about, you see a lot of African-American were upset about those forty acres of land, and a mule their ancestors were promised, but some of them never did receive, and those who did received that offer, lost it all to those white sheets riders of the night, who the land belonged to at first before the Civil War.

"After the north defeated the South, they confiscated the land from the white slaves owners, and divided it among the ex-slaves, as an incentive for their participation in the Civil War, helping the North to defeat the South, and that reason along caused a lots of southern whites, to hold a prejudice grudge against black people, organizing the Ku Klux Klan to take back their land."

Another white man spoke out. "I think it's the white men who is being discriminate against today, look at all of those black professional athletes, dominating most of the sports events, that were once controlled by white men, those black athletes are getting rich, grabbing themselves white women to marry.

"Because they think white women are princesses, with high quality prestige, among women of other ethnicities, race or skin colors whatever category, you want to put them in, and that what piss me off. I'm a blue-collar worker. They are living in big house, driving around in expensive cars, committing crimes, that are being looked over by the police, because of their popularity and athletic abilities."

Ulrica replied impudently, "You are wrong about that, mister, every professional black athlete doesn't take to white women for partnership, and those who have chosen white women for their spouses. I'm quite sure it happen, because they were in love with each other, and from the talk among you, Caucasian men, I think you fear, that if a black man, is given a fair chance, to learn the skill of any profession existing.

"He will do a better job than his counter-part, and you shouldn't worry about that, as long as there more Caucasian in the United States, white men, the majority of them will remain in dominating positions, like the white- collar jobs, even blue-collar workers, more white men are employed than blacks.

"A lot of you men are ex-military, veterans of foreign wars. Some of you have fought, side by side with black guys, who have save some of your lives or vice-versa, get back here in the United States, and let prejudice take its place. Black and white men in this country need one another, and you can live together like brothers."

Another man spoke out. "To be a Caucasian lady, campaigning to be the governor of this state, advocating equality for black people, trying to put them in the positions of white people. I say that's reverse discrimination. You are trying to put black people in our places, by the way, your husband is black right." Ulrica replied, "Yes, he is, speaking of his ethnicity, but I fell in love with his personality, because he's an intellectual man, with good common sense, overlooking the color of people skins conditions.

"And may I advise you, not to think stupid, because I'm married to a black man, doesn't mean I'm promoting interracial relationship. I want to see every citizen treated equal in this country. I see nothing wrong with two people of different gender regardless of their ethnicity, dating, socializing or marrying each other in this country, because the United States was built by people migrating here from different places, it is a melting pot, for people of different nationalities, to come and become American citizens."

Ulrica had her security people stationed among her white male audiences, keeping things under control, just in case someone wanted to act bold. A few of them did, and they were apprehended, and escorted out of the building to jail. One man shouted out, "It is contagious for white people to be prejudice against blacks. Although, we tried to hide it, in this modern day society, but such social and ethnical attitudes, still exist among the minority of white people, this feeling of hatred or fear witnessed by them, in the presence of black people is known as Negrophobia, because their physical appearances are so much different, and their style of living was once inferior to that of white people."

Ulrica replied, "That is ridiculous, prejudice is not like a disease, that can be spread, it is taught by racially stupid people, who have been mislead by some bad rumors, that have been spreading all of these years. If you are intelligent, you can see the difference of a person's appearance, has nothing to do with his or her character, as a human being.

"If given an equal chance, most black people would live a decent and prosper lives, just like the educated whites, who are earning that type of money, to buy what they wanted, and for the word Negrophobia, and its meaning was created by an insane lunatic bigot."

Another man spoke out on black militant groups promoting hatred toward white people, trying to under minds white politicians, evoking black revolution, causing racial riots and other disturbance, contributing to the movement of black power. He claimed that these groups of black people were asking for segregation to be reinstated, requesting that the blacks have their own states of this nation, with the equality to do business with other countries of their choice. This action shows that there are some black people just as prejudice toward whites as whites toward blacks.

Ulrica responded to his accusation. "Yes, I have read the history of such group of people, most of them are in prison, because their organization was disrupted by the federal government. Their members were disarmed, arrested and sent to prison, and the rest of them went underground as a check and balance against the existence of white militant groups."

There was a white man, who spoke out from a guilty conscience. He told the audience how his father taught him, and his siblings to dislike all people who weren't of his ethnicity, specially black people, and after he got older, he found out that his father, had produced a family of siblings by his black mistress, and he met his half brother and sister, while attending an integrated high school, during his senior year. This was something Ulrica was familiar with, how parents can keep such a secret, about their interracial child or children.

Another man spoke out about people being prejudice, because of the skeletons in their closets. They are trying to hide or deny. He confessed about his mother taught him to be prejudice against black people, and at the same time, she was cheating on his father, her husband with their black yard worker. His father came home unexpected from work, and caught his mother in bed with this black man, and she screamed rape. The black man was arrested and found hanged in his jail cell the next day.

Another guy spoke out about the racial fights that broke out among black and white students, during the forced integration of public schools. He became prejudice toward black students, because they would fight the white students as a revenge for what happen to their ancestors, during slavery and the reconstruction era of the United States, when black people were looked on as an inferior race.

Ulrica replied, "Yes, I read about some of those racial fights between black and white students, forced to go to school together, integrating the south's school system. The unjust part of those situations were the black students got expelled from schools for the rest of the year, causing them not to graduate, if they were in the twelve grade, because of racial altercation ended up as a physical fight, preventing them from achieving a high school education, and there were some white students, starting fights on purpose, to get the black students expelled from school."

Another white man replied, "In this country, the majority rules, and as the census goes, there are three times as many white people in this country as blacks, and the constitution of this country was written to protect its white citizen." Ulrica replied, "The constitution of this country was written to protect all of its citizens, the majority may rule, but the minority has rights. I don't want to make this a black and white issue. I want to be the governor for all the state of Oregon citizens. No matter what their nationalities, religions or ethnicities maybe, if you become my constituency, and elect me to the governor's seat. I will be obligated to serve the people of this state with equality, bring in bigger businesses with better paying jobs, clean up this state politic, and treat people equally, regardless of their skin condition. I will govern this state with the charm of a mother."

Ulrica campaign strategy had alleviated most of her male Caucasian audience's ethnocentric attitudes, but there were those reluctant to vote for her, because she was a Caucasian lady with a black husband. They thought that she would be impartial toward the dominating positions held by the white citizens. Ulrica being an Italian-Puerto-Rican American woman with biracial children, she had a callosity time convincing these men that her political moderate party has an innovated way of governing the state of Oregon, that will be appreciated by all of its citizens.

Ulrica came home exhausted from debating with victory, campaigning diligently and lecturing convincingly, to win the conservative bias attitudes of those white men, reluctant to vote for her as governor.

She would always take care of her motherly duty, after a day work, showing love and care for her children, spending time to talk and listen to them, before giving them a bath for bed. Although we had a live in nanny, Ulrica wanted Bobby J. and Victoria to know the different between their mother and nanny. She would give Marcie days off with pay, whenever she wanted to spend time alone with her family.

This particular night, I was lying on the reclined couch, reading the newspaper, when Ulrica came into the den, walking toward me with a drink in each of her hands, eyes full of lust, and a sexy smile on her face, as she came to me giving me a drink, while laying on top of me, whispering these words into my ear. "Darling, I had a long frustrating day, and the only way I survived it, was by thinking of you, doing you husbandly duty, making long, hard, hot passionate love to me over and over again. Are you capable of extinguishing this hot horny fire burning wildly between my thighs."

I replied, "That is my duty as your husband, soothing you as my wife with prolonged passionate loving." She began kissing my lips with tender foreplay technique, causing my penis to stiffen with an erection, pressing against her crotch, and she moaned softly into my ear. "Hhhoo, ahaha, now I feel what you are talking about, that old boy down there, is ready to log itself inside of me, come on baby let's get into the Jacuzzi." She took my hand, and led me to the Jacuzzi. I'm walking so close behind her, until each step she would take; her soft round butt was bouncing against my crotch, before we got to the Jacuzzi, we were taking our clothes off.

Ulrica possessed everything I desired about a woman, with such good quality, as my wife, she gave me compromising advises, and she always listened, whenever I had something to say, and she can carry on such an inspiring, ears pleasing, hearts influencing, and minds convincing conversation, as a politician, she is a decision making lady, and she is my emotional co-coordinator, knowing that I was addicted to women, with great physical appearances, cute eyes pleasing to see faces, with salaciously stimulating bodies figures, and intellectual attitudes, but she is my Miss Pulchritudinous, keeping herself in tip top physical shape, even after giving birth to two babies, a boy and a girl, and she still looks, just as smooth and firm as a virgin.

She knows what it takes to keep her body looking great, and her hygiene is stimulatingly fresh, and sweet-smellingly clean. Whenever Ulrica wanted to seduce me intimately, she would get this way, wearing her favorite perfume that will stimulate my olfactory nerve, like the best aphrodisiac in the world, making me hungry to make love to her, and when we are sexually indulging, it is artistic to witness, such performance between her and me, this is lovemaking to the highest degree, finishing sweaty wet and enervatingly feeling great, as our last thrills of life linger fadingly away.

As a mother, Ulrica is always showing love and affection for her children, and she is also a discipline mom, teaching our daughter, and son right from wrong, while they are young, and they know when they are wrong, and I learned not to interfere, during her discipline mood, unless I feel, she's being sort of rude, and need to cool her attitude, because she is a politician, and she can be callous, when it comes to discipline people as criminals. She even arrested her family members, so we did agreed, as a part of our parenthood technique, try not to interfere with each other disciplining technique, unless it's affecting our feeling, how our children are being treated, but Bobby J. and Victoria were pretty well discipline. Marcie was doing an excellent job as a nanny, but they still have their little altercation with each other, and I'm mostly taking side with baby girl, and Ulrica defends little Romance, talking about sleeping on the couch, if I don't be nice.

Since we are rearing a family of siblings, our lovemaking technique can't be as exotic, as it uses to be. After having sex, we have to sleep in our pajamas, this was something Ulrica insisted on doing, just in case Bobby J. or Victoria get up early, and run into our bedroom. Ulrica said it would be more respectful, if they never see us lying together in bed naked, so sometime I lock the door to our bedroom, because it turns me on, waking up in the morning, seeing her beautiful nude body, lying next to mine.

Whenever Ulrica had a rough day of campaigning, she seems to come home in a disgusting mood, somewhat frustrated and half way humiliated. I could tell by the way she looked and talked, that it was a signal for me to comfort her with my romancing ability, drowning her with complimentary hugs and kisses, speaking words of encouragement into her ear, enhancing her confident with self-esteem to prevail with victory over her oppositions. Assuring her confident with a night of sexual romance, most people after experiencing an orgasm, during sexual intercourse, become debilitated and sexual enervated, after feeling intensified great, as this thrill of life linger away, which seems to revitalize Ulrica mental, emotional and physically.

Now Ulrica was trying to win the votes of this state's black female citizens, some of these women were showing just as much prejudice toward the interracial relationship, between black men and white women, as the white men did, but Ulrica stood strong, and spoke firm against racism, while visiting some of the state's low income housing areas where the ghettoes were developed into slums.

The residents of poor minorities people, mostly black women serving as single parents, victims of drug abuse, children dropping out of high school, teenage girls are getting pregnant on purpose, just to get welfare help, teenage boys becoming gang members, committing crimes for the fame of doing jail time, until they reach the age of an adult, most of their adolescent lives were institutionalized.

People in the minority communities throughout the United States were reluctant to vote, because of the different conniving and crafty schemes pulled on them, claiming they were ineligible to vote, in an inappropriate way, with letters to their addresses or flyers being passed out throughout their communities, mainly the black citizens, frustrating them with such mendacious information, accusing them as being ineligible voters, if they were on welfare and not working, because only working and tax paying citizens were eligible to vote. Another wrongful information was if someone had been arrested, and did jail time as a misdemeanor made him or her ineligible to vote as citizens, even if they received a traffic ticket will prevent them from voting as American citizens. These unfair tactics were motivated by racial people, trying to eliminate black people from voting in different elections, so that the right politicians can't get in the position, to make life in this country livable for all people.

Ulrica was trying to assure these less fortune citizen, suffering under this country's economic system, that she can help them to better their living conditions, if they vote in the effort of electing her to the governor's seat, she would give them a chance to move out of the projects or poor establish ghettoes, into a higher class of living.

If she's elected as their state official, she will create state funded program that would assist poor people to take a higher step in the class of living, by taking the state's surplus to rescue the poor, and give them a better opportunity to live decent. She will create a system that will help unfortunate parents and their children to compete with the more fortunate citizen of this state, especially for the children sake.

Ulrica held a conference with a group of unprivileged black women, who have suffered the bad part of life, drugs abusers, burned out prostitutes, single parents on welfare with a group of children, don't know who their fathers are, and don't care, because they think this society, put black people off in the ghettoes, to keep them uneducated, crimes infested and poor, with the military offering those who are qualified, a chance to change their lives style. Most of these women are not registered voters, and Ulrica was telling them how important it was for them to register and become voters. It would give them the right as constituency, to elect the person of their choice, to represent them as their political figure. Who can suggest laws to be written and make decisions that can improve their styles of living.

One sassy looking black lady asked Ulrica why white women on welfare receive certain kind of public assistant denied to black women, and why the poor white folks don't live in the ghettoes with the poor black people, since this supposed to be an integrated system of living.

Ulrica assured these ladies, if she is elected as their governor, all citizens of the state of Oregon, whether they are Black, White, Hispanic, Asian, or whoever seeking public assistant, and are qualified to receive it, will receive the full benefit, because that is why we tax people, and have state lottery existing, so that this state have enough money, to help the less fortunate people, to better their living conditions.

One black lady spoke out with a militant attitude, inquiring about white women and black men relationship, claiming that most of the white women, who are indulging intimately with black men, are considered by white men as being low class white trash, who have dropped out of high school, dating black men, because they want to be cool, participating in orgy, ended up getting pregnant, and claiming the blame on the guy, who she enjoyed having sex with the best, as the father of her child, trapping him to marry her or get on welfare, and have him pay child support.

Another black woman spoke out boldly. "Yeah, she is right, a lot of these black men are stupid, acting like fools behind those low class white bitches, who have been victims of incest by some of their male family members, causing them to feel degraded and inferior, and as the result of their family mistrust, they feel more secure with black men with hoodlums, thugs, and criminal attitudes, knowing they are going to end up spending most of their lives in jail, and when they do, they will find another man to spread their legs to."

Ulrica didn't appreciate hearing such accusations, these black women were making, about white women and black men, and out of reluctance, she spoke like this. "I hope we can look at the relationship, between white women and black men, as two individual people of different gender, showing love and affection for each other, without finding the issue, of their ethnicity to separate them.

"There is nothing wrong with two people sharing intimate interest with each other, whether they are Black, White, Asian, Hispanic or other, no matter what their nationalities or ethnicities maybe, a man and a woman are made to indulge with each other as human being, and as far as incest goes, any person can be a victim of such mistrust."

Ulrica heard this coming from another black lady. "Yeah, that is easy for you to say, because you are married to a wealthy black man, with a college education, and a money making occupation. Just like in college, a lot of those black sports players, become professional athletes, making big money, then they run and marry a white woman, trying to look impressive."

Ulrica replied, "On the contrary, I used my money and my expertise to assist my husband into his money making profession. In order for this country to survive as a world leader, black and white people will have to stop showing prejudice against each other existence."

Another lady spoke out audaciously. "I don't have a beef with white women, but I do have something against those short ass Asian people, and I don't appreciate how the United States operate immigration, when it comes to bringing foreign people into this country, and giving them better opportunity, to receive higher prestige of living, than their own naturally borne poor black citizen.

"A lot of black men went over there and lost their lives, fighting for a cause that wasn't our, and when everything was over with, the U.S. government brought those Asian people to the United States, and put them in better places to live, than most of the black military men, who fought over there, returning home poor, and economically forced to live back in the ghettoes, some ended up in prison, because they couldn't get a job, retrieved as criminals robbing, stealing, killing and dope dealing, also living on the streets as homeless people."

Ulrica regretfully replied, "That is an issue, I will look into that seriously, and if that's a fact, that black veterans haven't received the same treatments with benefits like other veterans of foreign wars, then this state shall do its job, to see that black veterans are treated just as equal, and with respect as any other ex-military men, who served their country honorably, and I will inspire the federal government to investigate, any accused negligence on their parts against black veterans."

This heavy set, homely looking black woman started talking ghetto bold about black and white women relationship replying. "Yes, these old cunt faced, Caucasian women, cunnilingus ass Niggers make me sick, with their bitch asses, when they were with black women, they physically abused them, and now they with these white women, treating them like princesses." Another woman spoke out. "Shut up, bitch! You are pissed off with jealousy, because of the fact that your little white bi-sexual bitch, who was shackling up with you, left your dike ass for a black man. Now you are trying to make her jealous, by dating a white man." This big lady was shock, to hear the truth, spoke to her by another black woman, and these two ladies were about, to get physical with each other, but Ulrica a security people intervened.

That when Ulrica recognized the lady speaking for black men, was Odessa, one of Ulrica junior high school mate, who gave Ulrica a black eye, when they got into a fight with each other. Then this other big black women recognized Odessa from being in jail, Odessa worked as a security guard there, and she was moon lighting as security personnel for Ulrica campaign manager.

After this big black lady back down her bluff, everything quiet down. Ulrica approached Odessa, and she reacquainted herself with Odessa, who gave her a friendly hug. They ended up having coffee together, talking about their lives, and Ulrica offered Odessa a job as the head of her campaign security team.

Ulrica did some campaigning throughout the Asian and Hispanic communities, assuring them as their governor, she would show more interest in their existences as concerned citizens of the state of Oregon. Ulrica advocated that the Asian and Hispanic people have contributed great blending cultures to this society. She talked to different social groups of these communities, answering their questions about her form of governing.

She gave them her promissory oath for their votes, that she would see that they will receive equal opportunity for fair housing, jobs, health and financial assistant, also a better opportunity for their children to receive quality education. Ulrica stated that she would hire more minority people of different ethnicities to work in her administration, if she is elected as the governor of their state.

Ulrica did some campaigning to a group of black men, who felt that they were being neglected by big businesses, especially when it comes to receiving white-collar jobs, and some of these men had something to say about the justice system, against black criminals receiving more harsh penalty for committing the crime as equal as those done by white men, who would ended up being placed on probation or pay a fine, whereas for the black men, they will be sent to prison for a long term sentence, causing them to lose their right to vote as citizens.

Another black man spoke out. "Prison is a way for this society to enslave black people. We are suffering under this country economic pressure, denying us jobs to work for a living, seduced us with illegal activities, so that we can be arrested and go to prison, as a mean of eliminating us, from good paying jobs competitions. It's a fact that each state of this nation's prison houses 75 percent of more black inmates, instead of justice in this country, black men get rejected."

Another black man spoke out about black men who served in this country's militaries, and how some served with honor, contributing to every war the United States fought, and there was emphasis stressed, concerning the Vietnam conflict, and how many white American, evaded the draft by refusing to serve their country, in a military conflict in Asia. A lot of those Caucasian men fled the United States, gave up their citizenship, to become residents of other nations, such as Canada, Mexico, some countries of South American and Europe, and when the United States pulled out of Vietnam, all of those draft dodgers were pardon, and they were welcome back to this country with open arms. One of those draft dodgers became a politician, and ended up in the position of being the United States president for eight years straight.

While a lot of black Vietnam veterans were denied jobs, some of them ended up living on the streets as homeless victims or serving time in prison for the crimes they committed, trying to make a living.

Some of these black men claimed that most of the white men in this society are insecure by the increasing competitions the black American men are giving them, with equal opportunity to compete, and given a chance to prove on the average, they are better athletes, participating in different sports activities, and with the proper training, and given a fair chance to compete, black men will dominate other professions held by white men.

Another black man expressed his opinion why white businesses are reluctant to hire black men respectfully, because white men fear that if more black men are hired to work in the positions with prestige. They will increasingly win the hearts of white women, that why the few blacks in those positions possess homely appearances, but despise their prejudice attitudes toward black men working in white-collar positions, more and more white women are sharing their lives with them.

Another black man expressed his thoughts on the reason why more black men are found in prison than any men of other ethnicities in these United States, not just because of the color of their skins, it's the romance ability of their manhood, physically capable of making women feel good. He received some laughs from the other black men with that remark, as he continued that there are some jealous hearted white men in the position to criminalize black men through a political scheme to incarcerate them through a long confinement as an effort to eliminate the competitive threat black men are giving them.

Ulrica assured these black men that she will, if elected governor of the state of Oregon, look into such allegation, they are accusing the white men are doing to discriminate against them achieving prestige, because they are in the positions to do so. She was faced with questions about black military veterans, receiving fewer assistants than white veterans. Ulrica spoke her concern about the role black men played in this country, and as their governor, she will see to it that black men are treated just as equal as white men, being that they all are U.S. citizens.

Another black man spoke out about some black military men stationed in foreign countries, and meet some of the ladies in those places. They decided to get marry and live in those countries, instead of returning to the United States with their Caucasian wives, because interracial marriages are more accepted in Europe, the home of the Caucasian race than the United States.

Another man spoke directed to Ulrica. "You are talking about true democracy, being married to a black man, will lessen your chance of achieving the governor's seat." Ulrica regretfully replied, "I'm determined to do what is right for all people of this state with the gift of true democracy."

Another black man spoke out against interracial marriage. "I personally think, if a black person marry a white person, he or she is disrespecting the struggle of their race, and their marriage will be dominated by their Caucasian spouse, because he or she will feel superior, because the color of their skins, that what make people visually different, the complexion of their ethnicities. The lighter the complexion makes a person live better, because this society is dominated by white people."

Each time Ulrica has to face a challenging group of people, utilizing her campaign strategy, convincing enough to win them over as her constituencies, enervates her mental, emotional, and physically. She comes home as a weary mother, and an exhausted wife, hungry for some family soothing comfort, and my rejuvenating advice.

After showing her mothering love to our two children with me by her side, cuddling them into her arms, taking time to play educational child games with them, together we watch television with the kids, before she put each of them to bed with a bedtime story to read.

Marcie again is given her few days off with pay, whenever Ulrica falls into her motherhood mood. This was Ulrica effort of releasing her political stress, and as my wife, I comfort her with my massaging technique to release her stress mental, emotional and physically, stimulating her intimate interest for some bedroom blissful feeling, as we lay wrapped in each other's arms, discussing what was going on with her quest for the governor's seat, and she was feeling more confident in her ability of winning it. After a couple nights of good sleep, Ulrica became rejuvenated full of political strength.

She got a chance to campaign to a group of Caucasian women, hoping to win them over as her constituencies. They talked about women rights to receive equal pay to that of the white men, doing the same type of jobs as them. Ulrica promised them, as their elected governing official, she will have any place of business investigated for pay discrimination against women of any ethnicity, and if such business is found guilty of this unlawful act, there will be a fine for them to pay for such discrimination.

One lady spoke about sex harassment to keep a job. Ulrica replied, "There is an existing law against sex harassment in the workplace. Any lady witnessing such abuse as this can sue for monetary reward, because women rights are rooted in the civil right law, and no woman has to put up with such unwanted treatment on the job."

Another Caucasian lady spoke out her concern about her black husband who keep losing his job, when his white bosses meet her, and wanted to make out with her, and she refused to sleep with them. This has happened three times, since they been married, on different occasion, by three different employers of her husband, at a company's party, banquet, and picnic, she was approached by her husband's boss complimenting her appearance, and propositioning her sexually, when she refused such intimacy, two weeks later, her husband gets lay off from his job, with the excuse of cutting back on man power.

She proclaimed, if she wanted to mess around sexually with a white man, she would have married one, not claiming to be prejudice against men of her own ethnical background, but she married the man who she loved, because of his individuality, not his ethnicity, and because his wife is an attractive Caucasian lady, they shouldn't found fault with him, because she was financially able to take care of her husband and herself, but he doesn't want it that way, and she will stand by him no matter what type of racial trouble facing them. Ulrica and this lady had something in common; intellectually attractive Caucasian ladies with black husbands, and the white men didn't appreciate that.

Ulrica applauded this lady's courage, and assured her as governor of that state, she will declare war against racism, because racial prejudice has no place in the United States today. No group of people has the right to spread hatred against any citizen of this country, no matter what his or her existence maybe. It is unconstitutional, and there is a law pending against racism, and she will enforce such a law.

Once again Ulrica heard a Caucasian lady complain about the harassment white women are receiving, mainly by white men and black women for dating or marrying black men. White men and black women have been producing color people since slavery, and today it is more accepted by this society for a white man and a black woman to indulge into an interracial relationship, than it is for black men and white women. White men think white women are violating their ethnical pride by indulging intimately with black men.

Another white lady confessed that when a white male coworker approached her for a date. She turned him down replying to him that she doesn't dates white men, she only dates black men, and this white guy took that as an insult, and told the rest of the Caucasian males, working at that company, and they begin giving her a hard time, passing her over for promotion, and she filed a discrimination sue against the company, for treating her inferiorly, because she dates black men.

Ulrica was asked an ultimate question concerning sexuality. A lady in the audience replied, "Do you think special privilege should be given to homosexual people, because of their condition, and do you think they should be given the opportunity to marry member of their own gender legally." Ulrica replied, "I'm heterosexual, and it is my moral and social belief, according to the norm, I grew up under, that homosexuality is wrong, condemned by the God of my belief."

I personally think it is sickness for people to sexually indulge with members of their own gender. Now as people and citizen of this country, homosexual are protected by the constitution of the United States' civil right laws, but to promote homosexuality, I think it is moral, social and legally wrong. We people of this country put too much emphasis on rearing our children with proper manners.

"Exposing them to homosexuality or telling them there is nothing wrong with it, is inappropriate for parents with good decency to do so. Now to think of insanity, the concept of this word can describe different levels or degree of such existence as be mentally ill, how can a sane person possesses the desire to have sex with a member of his or her gender. There has to be some type of mental deficiency or emotional mal-function, these people are suffering from, because we all know this is not a perfect world.

"So such mental or emotional illness can affect person sexuality or some type of physical defect of his or her sex organ can cause this type of lifestyle. There are different reasons, why people are homosexual, whatever the case maybe, there are rehabilitative programs, being established throughout this country with professional trained counselors, who can work with these people, and give them certain treatment that will converse their homosexual behavior."

Another lady spoke out. "Some people are ignorant to the existence of homosexuality. True homosexual people are intelligent human beings, and they know how to stay within their limit, when interacting with other people, but those delirious bi-sexual freaks, who are so ambiguous about their sexual preference of having sex both ways, are the cause of these deadly disease to occur, and spread throughout the homosexual and heterosexual communities, so as a man loving woman, I could never submit to the legality of homosexuality, but we know as human beings, they have such a right."

Ulrica heard another lady speak out on homosexuality. "Since lesbianism is more promotional and accepted by this society than the activities of gay men, do you think this will cause more heterosexual women to indulge sexually with other women from the curiosity or the belief that a woman can understand the emotional aspect of another woman better than a man." Ulrica replied, "Understanding how another woman feels, is totally different from indulging sexually with that individual."

Another lady replied, "I think the act of cunnilingus between two women is not as disgusting, as homosexual men having anus intercourse with each other or performing the act of fellatio." Ulrica replied, "I think homosexual activities are disgusting for any sane human being to participate in, it's just not a Godly thing to do, and as some of these people get older, they refrain from such insane activities.

"May I reiterate, this is not a perfect world, and homosexuality is an existence, we will have to live with, just like any other social, mental, emotional, and physical illness, a cure for it has to be found." Another lady asked Ulrica, does she thinks the increasingly spread of homosexuality will be such a threat to heterosexual, until there will be a worldwide war between these two sexualities.

Ulrica replied, "I hope not, because a worldwide war between sexualities or ethnicities will be a disaster to the lives of human beings. There are enough natural catastrophes that can destroy the existence of human beings, and we don't know what type of existence beyond life on earth. I think, we human beings are intelligent enough to live with each other, the diversity of ethnicities and sexualities can be accepted by any rational human being, because there is one thing we all have in common as human beings, and that is, we all were borne to die, and we should understand that death is the equality of all human beings."

An older lady spoke out. "I agreed with that statement you just made, and as far as other existences, I believe homosexual people are really aliens from out of space. They can't produce babies, that is the purpose of having sex to increase the population."

Another lady spoke out loud. "I don't know about all of that, I have sex, because it makes me feel great, there is nothing that can make a woman feel as nice as the thrill of life, erupting between her thighs and spreading that intensified joy throughout her body, vibrating her heart, that why they call it making love, because such a feeling, cause people to get emotionally involve with each other, heterosexual and homosexual, both can get a nut or experience an orgasm, without the help of the opposite sex, I'm talking masturbation, self-indulging, you don't need a wife or a husband, because living with other people ain't nothing but trouble, it is hard for people to get alone with each other."

Ulrica replied with a disguising smile, "Whatever it may be, elect me to this state's governor's seat, and I will do my best to make life for every citizen to appreciate. "

Ulrica hold a conference with a group of humanitarians, praising them for being so kind and generous with their giving as philanthropies, because they believe that man's sole moral obligation is to work for the improved welfare of humanity. She tried to encourage them to be more consider toward the hungry and homeless people, asking them to donate more money to feed the hungry people of that state, and monetarily help to establish places for the homeless to stay, because there are more stray people on the streets, these days than there are cats and dogs, because is a law to put stray cats and dogs to sleep, kill them by legal injection, can't do people that way.

As governor, Ulrike pledged to outlaw people sleeping on the sidewalks of cities business districts. The sights of them seem indecent to be citizens of a country as rich and powerful as the United States. That is why people with money pay taxes, so that the money would be used to help those in financial need.

Ulrica stated that old abandoned buildings, apartments complex, and houses can be renovated with tax money to shelter the homeless, and if those homeless people are too proud to accept an understanding help, then they will have to sleep in the parks, because sleeping on cities' streets will be against the state's law.

Ulrica also pledged as governor, the state will create jobs that will train people to perform such occupational skill, and she will give big businesses a tax break, if they move into this state, and hire people to do, on the job training, so that they can become better skilled workers.

Ulrica next campaign challenge was to talk to the medias better known as the communication businesses such as; newspaper companies, television stations, magazines, radios, any business that have relationship with the public. Her main concern for addressing the medias was to ask them to be more of mediators and not instigators toward her effort in seeking the governor's seat.

She was putting forward effort to encourage the medias to do the jobs, that are expected of them, and that is to assist in resolving problems that occur between conflicting parties, report the news as fact, and not exaggerate it for high rating, problems that occurs between businesses and the consumers, should be known to the public, and solutions between politicians and their constituencies, by bring to their attentions, that the promise they made to their constituencies should be kept.

Ulrica campaigned for the votes of the elder people. She spoke of encouragement to the elder citizen, and asked that the young and middle aged people show respect and concern to the existence of those who have lived to reach that golden age of survival, and that the state should assist more, in the welfare of its elderly citizens, by providing free health care for the old and poor, nursing homes with modern medical technology for the emergency of older people.

Ulrica addressed a group of young citizen eighteen through their twenties years of age, outside of requesting for their votes. Ulrica spoke words of encouragement to them, challenging them to take a positive stand in life, by accepting the responsibilities of intellectual citizens, try to make as few mistakes in life as possible, choose the occupation that will offer them a life time security, also put forward their best effort in choosing the right compatible spouses. Someone his or her love will grow stronger throughout a lasting relationship, and be responsible parents by rearing their children with the wisdom of life. She also promised free education beyond the twelfth grade, two years of continuing education, the state would pay for such enlightenment.

Ulrica campaigned to the middle aged citizen by asking for their advice on what they think the governor of this state should consider improving for the state's future. She even went to different religious denominations congregational service, to ensure the citizen of the state of Oregon, that she will serve as their governor, with the goodness of God in her heart. Some of these religious people seem somewhat skeptical about electing a dark- complexioned Caucasian lady of an interracial marriage with biracial children as the governor of their state.

As a family visiting these different religious denominations, we observed that Sunday was the most segregated day of the week. Diversity of the citizen from different ethnicities, and their nationalities was lingering like a racial illness moving under a slow process of being cure, and Ulrica's goal as governor was to put this process into a faster and more accepted mood of life. Ulrica campaign slogans were people make money, money doesn't make people, it can only be used to influence people decisions, ask what your state can do for you, and in return, you can do more for your state. As a candidate for the Moderate Political Party, Ulrica was considered the underdog, against her opponents a well-known Democrat and Republican.

A week before Election Day, Ulrica did what she usually would do, during a rough campaign conference. She retrieved into the mood of a loving and caring mother, to our son and daughter, and as a sexy wife, keeping the home fire burning, to enhance our relationship as spouse, and the parents of Bobby J. and Victoria, giving our nanny a week paid vacation, so that she can show her motherhood attitude to our children, and delight our bedroombedroom, each night with a sexual appetite.

The day after election, it was official that Ulrica unprecedentedly defeated her two opponents: Bill Richardson, the incumbent Republican, running for re-election to the governor's seat, who was disappointed for losing out to a woman, and Paul Good law, the county commission, and a well known Democratic politician, couldn't believe that she defeated him also. There was a party thrown to celebrate and congratulate Ulrica on her victory to the governor's seat.

At the victory party, while dancing with the new governor of Oregon, in my arms, I whispered into her ear, "What the husband of a female governor is known as." She smiled with this reply. "Her husband and the father of her children." I was somewhat surprised to hear that.

Ulrica was three months pregnant, when she was sworn in, as the governor of the state of Oregon, she took her responsibility with the heart of a female lion, facing the problems of this state head on, increasing the numbers of law enforcers and teachers, throughout the state with a 15% pay increase, hiring people with the quality of great teachers and the righteous courage of great policemen. The public schools classes were lower in the numbers of students attending, so that each child would have an equal chance to learn more, and more money were being spent to enhance the state's educational system, and less on prisons.

More police officers were patrolling the areas of high crimes with more minority officers, putting criminals out of business in the low economic communities. Crimes and punishment were being taught in schools at three different levels, the basic was taught in the third grade. Sixth graders learned the mediocre stage of this course, and the ninth graders took the advance course of crimes and punishment, it was mandatory for the students to take these courses, as a way of alleviating the crime rate, and it did.

Ulrica wasn't satisfied with the crime rate committed by those heinous criminals, so she made a solution to that problem, by executing a death certificate, ordering all people on death row in prisons, to be killed within a year. She gave their lawyers a year to appeal this state's new law, stating that it will save the taxpayers money, from feeding and housing prisoners who were sentenced to die.

Ulrica gave birth to our third child, and second son. She named him Edmond T. Wilson. The T. stands for Terrell in memory of my father. After her maternity leave, Ulrica returned to work as a proven leader. She didn't back down, and the people on death row, cases were re-investigated, before their lives were taken, and there were a few people on death row, were found innocent, after the re-investigation brought forward new evident proving their innocence, and the state pay them for their mistake. One man didn't want to accept the state money. He praised the governor for a job well done.

Ulrica saw that a law was passed against racism, making it illegal for any a group of people to public march in protest against the existence of any other citizen of this country. Racial name-calling was a criminal offend, if proven guilty, the accused would have to pay the plaintiff a fine or do jail time. Ulrica's law was opposed by group racial of oppositions, marching in protest of this law, stating it is unconstitutional, violating their freedom of speech. The police arrived on the scene. This group of opposition resisted the arresting officers, and a physical confrontation occurred which led into a riot. The National Guard was called in the restore order, and these oppositions were arrested for the crime they committed, and those who participated in this racial related crime, who weren't a citizen of this country, were deported.

One night Ulrica and I were having one of our usual bedroom conferences on the crime of rape. She was wandering should there be a law implementing the castration of a rapist. I replied, "That should lower the crime of rape, down to the ground, then there would be a lot of minority men, walking around here penis-less. A lady can say anything, when she is mad or frustrated.

"There is a controversial about date rape, if no means no, how far did she let him go, before saying no, most ladies can experience an orgasm through foreplay, dry sex, then they want to quit, leaving him with a stiff erection, and the thought of her teasing him, causes him to force it in, against her resistance or maybe she submits to having sex with him, and he blows his rock and stop, leaving her wet and insulted, by having sex without experiencing the thrill of it, and she becomes frustrated, and call it rape.

"A man will have to have an alibi, before lying between a woman's thighs, and the lord knows a lot of black men have died, back in the days from, the mendacious accusation of rape, by being caught between the legs of white ladies, and to protect their guilt, they hollered rape quick, accusing him of taking it."

Ulrica replied, "This can be a complicated subject to discuss with my husband, but we are going to eliminate childhood rape for sure. There was a Caucasian man on death row about to die for the death of a child, he raped and killed his stepdaughter. She was nine years old, when he married her mother, and began to molest her at that stage of her life, and continued it, until she was twelve. She tried to tell her mother, what he was doing to her, but her mother just ignored the issue, until this girl turned twelve, her body had matured better than some eighteen years old girl, from his three years of molesting her.

"She had developed full breasts and butt. At the age of twelve, she began to experience her monthly cycle, that when he raped her physically, and threaten to kill her, if she told her mother or anybody else. Finally, this girl told her mother with physical proof that her stepfather been misusing her body as his sex object.

"Her mother and stepfather got into an altercation, and he attacked her physically, beating her unconscious, while this girl tried to help her mother fight him. He attacked her with his fists, punching against her face and body while raping her at the same time. He beat her to death, while laying between legs, copulating into her bloody dead body.

"When her mother regained her conscious, and saw her husband, raping the corpse of her daughter, she started hollering, screaming and crying while running into the bathroom with a cell phone in her hand. She locked the bathroom's door, and called the police, and her husband was arrested, while trying to break down the bathroom's door to kill her. Now lie's on death row, and within a week, he will never use his penis again, to piss or do anything else with it, nor will he breathe the breath of life, after midnight Thursday of next week, I'm put a stop to the rapist of innocent victims.

"Here is the scenario of this fatal rape case, the mother name is Everly Russell, brown hair, blue eyes, nice looking Caucasian lady, who was dating this Mexican man, an illegal alien from Mexico, who sneaked across the border, and came this far, selling illegal drugs. Pedro was his name. He was making good money, and Everly wanted him. She became his girlfriend. They were cohabiting with good living condition, until she got pregnant, and one of Pedro's friends got jealous of him, having a white girlfriend, who was pregnant by him, so one day some Drug Enforcement agencies came and took Pedro away.

"Everly never did see or hear anything from him since that day the D.E.A. took him away. She gave birth to his daughter, a cute blue-eyed biracial girl with Mexican and Caucasian blood. Everly named her daughter Melissa, and she was working as a single parent, trying to rear her daughter the best she can, without welfare help. Nine years later, Everly met this Red Neck Caucasian man, a construction worker by the name of Nelson. He started dating her for a while, looking at her daughter with horny eyes.

"Nelson asked Everly to be his wife, and she didn't deny his request, and said yes. Nelson got his wish, but his true mission was to sleep with Melissa, and he ended up killing her as a raped victim, after beating her mother. If I had my way, any adult found guilty of raping a child will die or lose his penis, that will be my decision."

I replied quietly, "You will be hell, if you was the president." She spoke seriously. "That will be my next attempt, if I succeed at this."

Ulrica's governorship was challenged by a group of homosexual people, demanding more right and privileges for gay people. Ulrica stood firm to her heterosexual belief and existence, making it a crime and punishment by law, if any person of the homosexual community is accused, and found guilty of infringing his or her sexuality belief or habit on heterosexual people unwelcomingly.

This law slows down the rapid spread of homosexuality. Some of these people returned back to their closets, after a riot of sexuality broke between homosexual people performed a protest march for the right to promote and recruit people to experience the life of their sexuality, breaking the law that was written against the spread of homosexuality, and a group of heterosexual people intervene with names calling, and fights broke out, gay bashing went on for about a week, causing many of these people to return to their clandestine activities, and they became more accepted by the heterosexual communities, when they refrained from making homosexuality a political issue, and became more secretly with each other as lovers, which was more appreciated by heterosexual men, because those homosexual women were putting them into stiff competitions.

Ulrica toughen her laws against juvenile delinquency, giving those deviating adolescent a lesson to learn, until they are grown. If a teenager committed an adult heinous crime, depending on the nature of it, and the amount of time the youth has been arrested. He or she can be convicted to serve as an adult for such a crime committed.

The state established a criminal institute for deviating youth, who refuse to conform to society's norms, from the age of ten to the age of eighteen. They were sentenced to a military type training facility, for a certain amount of months or years, until they reached the age of eighteen. Then they would be transferred to an adult criminal institution, if the crime they committed were that severe. Their daily activities will be five hours of classroom study courses, five hours of work detail, and five hours of physical disciplinary training, six hours of sleep or rest and three hours for preparation between each section.

Two juvenile delinquents challenged Ulrica's death penalty policy. These two teenage boys were sixteen years old apiece, and committed a crime to the first degree. They went inside of a church, one Sunday's morning, during the devotion of this congregation, shot and killed their ex-gang member and his girlfriend, plus the preacher of this church, when he confronted them for committing such a heinous sin in the house of the Lord.

To show this preacher, they didn't care about the house of the Lord, they shot him to death, before firing a few round of bullets into the congregation, wounding a few of them as they stampede out of the church, running for their lives.

These two young criminals took the preacher's car to get away in, and the first police to arrive on the scene; they ambushed her with multiple bullets wounds, while she was driving up to the scene in her patrol car. Bullets went through the windows and body of the police's car into her body, causing her to lose control of her vehicle, and it crashed into a building, killing her instantly.

While these two young killers evaded the other pursuing police's cars at a high speed chase, in the dead preacher's vehicle, which overturned while they were speeding around a steep curve of the road. The car flipped over four times, before crashing against a tree. The two teenagers were trapped inside the wrecked car unconscious and bleeding from their injuries. When the policemen arrested them at gun points with the help of the rescue men, cutting through the wrecked car, freeing them from being trapped inside.

They were taken to the hospital under heavy police security. After receiving treatments for their injuries, they were put in jail without bond bail. While these two youths were in jail, boasting about the crime they had committed. The District Attorney was asking for the death penalty, and Ulrica advocated that these teenagers should die for the crime they committed. One of these young murderers made this comment about the state deciding to give them the death penalty. "That bitch ass governor must be on her period, talking about giving youths the death penalty."

That statement made by him, pissed Ulrica off, and she advised the prosecuting attorney, how to present this case to the jury, with enough evident, so that these two heartless juvenile delinquencies will receive the death penalty.

During the trial of these teenagers, the motive they had for killing two other youths, a preacher and a female police officer was presented to the jury with four counts of first degree murder pending against them. The two young killers names were Tony Bliff, a sixteen-year-old Africa-American, who had a juvenile delinquent record, since he was nine years old for participating in gang fights, selling illegal drugs, and robbing old citizen.

Bliff's Caucasian partner name was Jason Longfellow, nearly seventeen years of age, who have been in and out of the juvenile court, since he was ten years old, for fighting his parents, shooting weapons in the city limit, participating in illegal gang activities, drugs dealing, and attempt to kill his girlfriend.

The two youths, Tony and Jason gunned down their ex-gang member, while he was singing in the church choir. He was a biracial male Japanese- Caucasian teenager, sixteen years of age, by the name of Chang Lee Williams, who was once a member of this three guys gang, and they pledged an oath to never desert each other. The three of them were constantly getting into trouble, expelled from school.

Then Chang Lee met this teenage Hispanic girl, by the name of Maria Garcia, who he fell in love with. He began to spend more of his time with her, and neglected his obligation to his gang members. Chang Lee started going to church with Maria, participating in different social activities with her, who was only fifteen years old when her life was stolen.

Reverend Leon Franklin, an African-American man, the pastor of this church, who was married with three children. He lost his life, while looking these two demons in their eyes, after they shot Chang Lee, and his girlfriend Maria to death with two fatal shots apiece, in their heads and chests. Reverend Franklin was killed, for denouncing these two killers, in the house of the Lord, and they gunned him down, and took the keys to his car from his pocket, while members of this congregation were running for their lives, some of them were shot and wounded, by these two killing youths.

Officer Carole McIntyre, a female Caucasian rookie on the police force, who heard the 911 call being dispatched over her patrol car's radio. She was so anxious to involve herself into some police action, until she reacted to fast, reluctant to wait on police back up, and lost her life, as the result of being in a hurry. Her car and body got shot up, causing her to lose control of her police vehicle, and it crashed into a building, killing her instantly.

Tony and Jason were in jail, boasting about the crime they committed made history, and Ulrica advised the prosecuting attorney to utilize such strategy, so the jury can see that these two adolescents, as menace to this society, and give them the death penalty for the crime they committed.

It was unprecedented in the state of Oregon or anywhere else in the United States, where two teenage boys were trailed as adults, and received the death penalty, within a year from the day, they were convicted, Tony Bliff and Jason Longfellow were put to death in Oregon state prison by legal injection.

Ulrica was there to witness such an execution. After that justify killing, the state of Oregon had the lowest crime rate in the United States, even misdemeanor was at a record breaking low.

Ulrica also implemented what she had promised to the poor people, there were different types of training programs set up throughout the state, teaching people on welfare different trades and skills for them to learn in order to enhance their occupational fields, and after they finished their work skill classes, they were immediately hired on the jobs for advance training, making the type of money for them to live more comfortable.

Ulrica also utilized the state's lottery surplus to set up a state wide head start program for children at the age of three to five, and it was nice to give a child the chance to learn and conform at an age that young. It also assisted parents on welfare to get a job while their children in head start.

More and more people began to move into the state of Oregon, because Ulrica had propositioned big businesses to locate in this state. It was a good position to conduct foreign trade. Such migration turned villages into towns, towns into cities, and cities into metropolitans. Ulrica was spending more time negotiating with state's politicians, having banquets and dinners, with Representatives and Senators, as a political fund raising effort, trying to get the majority of them to compromise with her proposition of legalizing marijuana, until she was neglecting her responsibility as a wife to me.

Ulrica was focusing on getting marijuana legalized through certain provisions, pending that the state of Oregon, will cultivate and manufacture this product, for the state to profit from the sale of it, to assist in its financial operation, and a person would have to registered as a marijuana smoker, in order to receive a certificate to purchase it, from the state of Oregon's house of spirit facilities.

Within three months, after this business were full established, facilities were still being built throughout the state and Oregon, and it was a multi-billion dollars business on the increase, with this type of money accumulating, the state of Oregon offered to lend enough money to help out the federal deficit.

Ulrica was facing a situation of how to legalize prostitution without insulting different religious denominations, and those citizen who value marriage life, and those believe in monogamy, knowing that sex is a natural act, and prostitution cannot be eliminated. It serve it purpose in different societies, and seems more legal for the rich to indulge in such a forever lasting activity, than the poor, and she knew there will be a problem, trying to tax the body of a person's sexual performance.

Prostitution is a victimless crime, and she was trying to have a law legislated to protect those who are jeopardizing their bodies and lives to profit from it, since sex is a need to most people, not marriage, then people should be able to have sex without obligation, and by legalizing prostitution, like they did gambling, it will lower the crime of rape, and alleviate the chance of catching different kind of sexual transmissible diseases. Sex education only stimulates those into wanting to have sex.

There was a heinous crime occurred, that caught people attention to make prostitution legal. There was this lunatic, serving as a serial killer, luring young female prostitutes walking the streets, with a large amount of money, he was offering them to go to his resident, and have sex with him. He was dressed decent and respectful. He owned a hog farm on the outskirt of town. He would pay these young hookers to get nude, as though to have sex with him, then he would sedate her with some type of unconscious causing drug, before taking her nude unconscious body to his hog's pen. He began to feed his hogs, that when he would throw the prostitute's nude body into the crowd of eating hogs, and they would eat her alive, just like she was a part of their feed.

This was a nasty and obscene scene to see, this man, masturbating while watching these hogs eat the flesh of a young lady's nude body. The pain from the hogs' teeth ripping into her flesh caused this lady to regain her conscience. She hollered and screamed momentarily, before she was dead and gone, eaten to pieces by these hungry hogs devouring her body.

There were twenty-seven prostitutions missing from these streets, and this serial killer name was Mike Wesley, a white-collar worker at a large computer firm. He drove up to accost two young ladies, walking the street one-day, dressed in sexual advertising attires. Mike couldn't get one lady to go alone with him without her girlfriend, so he decided to have sex with both of them, offering each enough money, to alleviate their reluctance to go to his resident.

When they got to his farmhouse, it looked nice inside. He gave them a drink each, while discussing sexual activities. Both ladies got nude, ready to perform sex with him, and then all of a sudden, they fell to the floor unconscious. Mike Wesley was a muscular built man, who stood about six feet three inches tall, driving a new luxury car. He took one of the prostitutes out of his house to the hogs feeding pen, when he threw her nude body into the crowd of feeding hogs, the second lady heard her screaming.

The second prostitute was half sedated. This drug wore off of her faster than Wesley expected, and she staggered out of the house, unaware that she was still nude, about fifty feet from where she was standing, she saw her friend's nude body, getting eaten by a group of hungry hogs, and this man was standing up with his clothes off masturbating. This young lady started hollering and screaming while running with no clothes on from this farm toward the highway, and she was moving like she was running a race.

This frustrated Wesley, because he was experiencing an orgasm, when she began to scream, startling him, and he started hollering at her with cussing words. "You motherfucking, death dodging bitch! Bring your pussy- selling ass back here! And die with your whoring ass friend." By the time Wesley rushed to put some clothes on, and get into his car to go after her, this lady was running down the highway nude, causing traffic congestion, some of the drivers pulled up beside her, trying to offer her a ride, but this prostitute was deliriously afraid, so she kept running and crying, until a state trooper's car pulled her over.

Wesley planned on running over this prostitute, claiming it an accidental killing, but by the time he got to her, she was getting into the state trooper's car. She was Wesley driving by, and started crying out loud, pointing at him replying, "That's him, he fed my girlfriend to his hogs." Wesley sped away, and was engaged into a police chase. Police's cars surrounded him, until he surrendered, and was arrested.

A team of forensic professional from the police force went to Wesley's farm, and examined his hogs' manures, and the evident was found in the hogs' feces, that he was feeding these missing prostitutes to his hogs, and at his trail, the way the second prostitute, described the way Wesley was masturbating, while watching his hogs eat up the body of her girlfriend. She was hyper sadden with her expression, and the jury found Wesley guilty, with twenty-seven counts of first-degree murder. He was sentenced with the death penalty. The state took his life within a year.

Ulrica legalized prostitution, in a way of establishing, a Social Surrogate Clinic, throughout the state of Oregon, for people seeking sexual entertainment, and this was a whopping money making business for men and women, especially those who were physically, eyes pleasing to see, with salacious bodies figures. This business made Oregon the wealthy state in the nation, causing other states to imitate this type of prurient operation. It almost put the pornography industry out of business.

Ulrica was praise for legalizing this business of intimacy, and sex crime was at a record breaking low, rape wasn't been done anymore, every now and then a guy may rape his girlfriend, because she got another boyfriend, or some lunatic rape a victim just to prove that he can do it.

Everything seems to be going Ulrica's way, except her marital situation, she found time to be a loving mother to our children whenever she could, but a wife to me, she began to act as though I didn't exist, so I approached he about the home fire burning situation, love me now or I will turn to another lady. She had too many excuses, from experiencing abnormal monthly cycle, not in the mood, because of this political challenging; she is facing as governor, trying to keep the citizen of this state vote of confident.

Ulrica left the state of Oregon for a meeting, concerning each state of the United States with the U.S. President, while she was away, I returned to our ranch with the children and house workers. Marcie was there with me, showing me the comfort I needed from such femininity. I came home one night bored from hanging out at the sport bar. Marcie was there to welcome me. We have played tennis together, and went horseback riding. She even gave me a stiff competition in a game of domino, after I taught her how to play the game. She was there comforting me with her femininity, taking the kids to the park, playing different games with them. She also gave me words of encouragement, that my wife still loves me, it just that she has a commitment to her constituencies.

It was a Saturday night, when I came home from the sport bar. Marcie had the weekend off to be with her boyfriend Pedro from the country Mexico. Marcie is also Mexican descent, but since she was borne in the United States, she considered her as a Chicano, Mexican borne in the United States, making her a Mexican-American, with beautiful caramel tan complexion, sexy legs, cute face, and a body figure that was stimulating to see, when she dresses flirtatiously, out on a date with her boyfriend.

It was about eleven o'clock that Saturday's night; the children were asleep in their rooms. I was in the party room, shooting a game of pool against myself, with music playing on the stereo, sipping on a glass of Cognac, when a car pulled up in the driveway. I heard a female and a male voice arguing in Spanish for a brief moment, and then the car drove off.

Marcie entered the house, she was dressed nice and elegantly. She walked into the party room, where I was shooting pool. She had a disappointed look on her face. I replied, "Sound like things didn't go too well for you, and your date tonight, I'm sorry about that." Marcie raised her head, and gave me a nice heart-warming smile replying, "That Pedro is a jerk, he accuses me of being in love with you, because I refuse to have sex with him tonight."

Marcie walked over to the bar, and made herself a drink. She took a deep swallow of it, and made a groaning sound, afterward she replied, "May I challenge you in a game of billiard?" I replied, "Yes, you may, but I will not show mercy for you." She replied in a sexy voice, "Mercy, is not what I'm looking for tonight." We shot pool together for a while, and she was putting me into stiff competition. We both were drinking, and a love song began to play.

Marcie surprised me, when she gently walked up to me caressingly, stimulating my olfactory nerve, with her sweet sexy smelling body; she looked into my eyes as she replied, "Tonight, being in the company of you, got me feeling warm and sexually hungry, she is neglecting your sexual need, and I feel as though it is up, to me to please you intimately, before you get desperate enough to go out there, and found yourself a slut."

Before I could respond, Marcie bad taken the pool stick from me, laying it on the table, and she embraced me with hugging arms, dancing romantically with me to the sound of this ears pleasing to hear love song, stimulating our sexual urge as the crotch of our bodies rubbed caressingly against each other. I received as erection, and she felt it bugling against my pant, rubbing against her thighs and crotch, showing that I was sexually interested. She began to feel, such a stimulating itch, causing her to seduce me farther with a passionate kiss. We were having dry sex, copulating against each other, with our clothes on, while hugging and kissing each other nice and firm.

Our breathing got louder, and Marcie began to moan, just as we began to undress one another, we were interrupted by little Edmond, crying in his sleep. I replied, "Hoop, the baby is crying." Marcie replied, "Don't worry, I will take care of him, go to your room, I'll be there soon." I went to the master bedroom, and took a shower, hoping that this overwhelming sexual desire, I'm witnessing, to indulge with Marcie intimately will soon leave me, but it didn't, while taking a shower, with cold water splashing all over my body, the thought of Marcie entered my mind, giving me an erection that wouldn't quit.

I had to have a cigarette to smoke, while I was dressed only in my bathrobe. I stood at the bedroom's patio slid glass doors with it open, smoking my cigarette, looking out, and up at the bright stars, lighting up the dark sexy sky, romance was in the air that night, then I felt the presence of another human being in the bedroom with me. As I turned around, I saw Marcie entering my bedroom, dressed in a sheer grown, and as nude as she wanted to be under it.

Marcie locked the bedroom's door before walking toward me, slowly removing the see through grown from her salacious body. Her lovely full and smooth breasts looked so delicious with erected nipples. My mouth was watering from the sight of them. This was the first time, I ever seen Marcie, looking so eyes pleasing to see, stimulatingly unique, as her grown fell to the floor, nothing but pure gorgeously glowing nude Chicano tan body, showing off the quality of her femininity to me.

Talking about a horny situation, the sight of her nudeness gave me an erection unbelievably, and it got bigger, as Marcie got close enough to de- robe me, and we embraced each other with lips sucking kisses, as though we were destitute lovers, hungry to sexually please each other intimate needs, talking about bodies hugging and rubbing against each other, tongue sucking and licking one another, while falling on the bed, it felt like we were falling in heaven.

After we finished with our foreplay technique, we indulged intimately into the lust of making love. I entered her body with such divine copulating skill, performing to please her overwhelmingly, as though she was my wife, who been away for a while. Off and on we filled each other with so much sexual fun. At the beginning of our sexual encounter, I was so turned on by her nude body, until I forgot to put a condom on, and whether she was using any type of contraceptive of her own, I wouldn't know, and she didn't tell me so.

From the time we began, until seven A.M., we were making each other feel sexually exuberant, witnessing such great intensified euphoric thrill, only the gratification of an orgasm can give, spreading such electrifying joy, throughout our bodies, causing Marcie to holler out her moans. I choked, to hold mine in, as we enervated each other through the act of intimately indulging, better known as making love, until we were debilitated, from sexually entertaining each other.

The next day, the cook and maid took Marcie place of caring for the children, because they knew, what went on between us, and thought it deserved Ulrica right, because she was neglecting her obligation to me as a wife. As we lay in bed, Marcie whispered these words into my ear. "A woman can tell when another woman has been sleeping in her bed, so after we finish sexually entertaining each other, wetting the sheet with the juice of our love, I will wash them completely clean."

Ulrica returned home a week later, she was glad to see her family, especially the kids, and I was glad to see her too, greeting her with hugs and kisses. Ulrica performed her usual mother duty, after neglecting her family for a certain amount of time, obligating to her constituencies by performing her political duty. She gave Marcie a few days off with pay.

We were a family again, just she, the kids and me spending weeks together, Ulrica even increased the flame of her home fire, performing her duty as my wife, making my bedroom's life nice. I didn't know whether she was crying or moaning, during our sexual performance, but she complimented me as being a great husband, and a superb lover, contributing to her ability to be a loving and providing mother, also strengthen her governing ability to bring such changing authority to the state of Oregon.

When Marcie returned to work, Ulrica would give her a suspicious stare, with a polite smile on her face, while observing her, talking to me, noticing how Marcie's eyes would brighten up with her smile, during our conversation. Marcie showed more freedom, while talking to me, with a laugh and a joke, every now and then, showing that our acquaintance was more than employer and employee, knowing that our intimacy was clandestine.

The state of Oregon had tripled its population within the two years of Ulrica's governorship there. Different types of professional sports teams had established themselves in this state, bringing in growing revenue. Ulrica popularity as a governing official grew tremendously, until she was nominated to run for the president of the United States, during the year two thousand and ten, and she became a candidate for such prestigious position. Her opponent was an elderly Caucasian man, representing the same political party as Ulrica. His name was Gowan Paul Washington, more conservative than Ulrica.

They utilized their campaign strategy against each other with the intelligence of respect for one another. Mr. Washington used the acronym of W.A.S.P. (white Anglo-Saxon Protestant) as a slogan, describing him as a member of the privileged, and established white upper middle class citizen of the United States.

His campaign strategy had people turning against Ulrica's improving democracy by spreading equality slogan. He had people remodeling their ethnocentric attitudes with the majority rules syndrome.

It was a close race, but by the blessing of his religious denomination, and members of his ethnicity, Mr. Washington prevailed over Ulrica with victory, proving that this country wasn't ready to elect a woman for the president of the United States with a husband of a different race and biracial children, who thought of themselves as being true U.S. citizen, produced by the blood of different ethnicities.

Ulrica felt that she was reneged on, by some of her women league members, for the pride of their ethnicity. I felt a release from her defeat, and just as I began to celebrate, of having Ulrica home as my wife, and mother of our children again, here comes Mr. Gowan P. Washington, pleasing with Ulrica to be his running mate, for the president of the United States, inspiring her with these words. "Mrs. Wilson, if you accept my offer as my vice-president, I promise you will be the most powerful vice-president in thehistory of this nation, and with your popularity advising my leadership ability, our opposing candidates will be defeated."

Ulrica teamed up with Gowan to run for the control seat of the United States, with a slogan such as this. "Make the right decision when you vote as United States citizen, send Gowan and Ulrica to Washington, D.C."

Some of their opponents spoke against the way Ulrica ran the state of Oregon, overlooking her political ability, making the state of Oregon the best place to live. Gowan and Ulrica took their campaign strategy on the road, throughout different states of this nation, and surprisingly most of the southern states initiated Gowan and Ulrica to be their presiding officials.

On Election Day, Americans were all eyes and ears, when the majority of this country's voters made their shocking decision, by unprecedently electing a Caucasian man as president of the United States with his female running mate being Latin-American, Italian-Puerto-Rican by blood as the vice-president of the United States.

I was shocked to hear such great news as this, and felt kind of guilty about my infidelity with Marcie, during Ulrica absent from our presence, campaigning for the second highest seat of authority in this country.

During the inaugurate ball, President Gowan Washington was so excited by becoming the United States president, going to different places, celebrating his victory, until he was politically enervated. Then another unprecedented event occurred, to this newly elected president of the United States.

After his overwhelmingly inaugurated celebration, President Gowan P. Washington die in his sleep, that night from anxiety, and here comes a Supreme Court Justice with all kind of security people, entering our house, breaking the sad and misfortunate news to Ulrica, the vice-president, in our bedroom, before swearing her into the position of the United States President, right there in our living room, of course she got formally dress, for this unexpected ceremony. Ulrica was sworn in as the President of the United States, before the citizen of this nation received the sad news, about the death of formal president Gowan P. Washington.

The moving people were there in our home, packing up our belonging for the White House of the U.S.A. After Ulrica received her oath, as president the United States, the United States Supreme Court Justice addressed me as first gentleman Wilson, Ulrica was the first female president of United States, another unprecedented occurring history making event.

After Ulrica was documented as the forty five president of the United States, it was urgent for her to address the nation, to express her condolence, to the family of formal president Washington, and gain confident from the citizens of this country as their leader, she expressed what was expected of her as president, and what is expected of them as American citizen, together they would make this country a world inspiration, and a much better place to live and rear a family with better jobs opportunity, enhanced education, cleaner environment, and military strength. She also proclaimed her focus on being more of a domestic president, but keeping awareness on foreign affair.

As the first gentleman of the United States, experiencing the political arena of Washington, D.C., I decided to walk around the inner part of this city, asking my Secret Service people to stay at a distance, so that the people won't notice or recognize me. I wanted to hear some gossiping, so I walked into a barbershop to get a haircut, and not long after I was seated, this black guy came into the barbershop, talking noise, instigating my situation. "Say, man, yah seen the new president, I ain't never seen a president that fine and pretty. She is intelligent too, one of those dark-complexioned Caucasian lady. I heard talk, that she is going to do for this country, no man president had ever done before."

"Yeah, I also heard that she was married to a Negro, hee-hee with four children or more, I bet that nigger thinks he's top shit, to be considered the first man of this country, that put him over those white folks and other people, and I will like to bust my big toe off into his ass hee-hee, if I ever see him." The people in the barbershop began to clear their throats.

I spoke to him ghetto bold and tough with my words. "You are a lying son-of-a-bitch, motherfucker, you rather fight a Grizzly bear with a switch, than to fuck with me." He looked at me with fear in his eyes, as my bodyguards came near. He replied, "Who are you? Oh, shit, Mr. Husband of the president, I'm sorry, sir, I was just talking shit, just another ghetto brother, about to let his mouth get his ass into trouble, please accept my apology." I told my security people to take a good look at him as I walked out of the barbershop.

Three months of her presidency, Ulrica and Marcie seen to be witnessing some type of morning sickness. When Ulrica said that she was going to be more of a domestic president, she wasn't kidding, she had already formulated a plan to stop immigration in this country, and for those people from foreign countries, living in the United States, she made it easier for them to apply forcitizenship, and within two years, they would be United States citizens. Human right was her main concern with the environment, clean air and flesh water, natural resource, forest, and consumers and businesses relationship.

Ulrica propositioned me to take this trip to Africa as a mission to improve their living conditions and relationship with the United States. Her brother Johnny invited me there to visit several countries of that continent, negotiating on becoming alliance with each other to show the rest of the world, Africa modernization will be their competition; social, technical, economic, military, agriculture and politically. As I prepared to take this trip, Marcie and Ulrica were trying to keep their morning sickness their secret. They and the children with Secret Service people, went to the airport with me to see me off, giving me farewell hugs and kisses.

Marcie's final words were whispered into my ear while she was hugging me. "You be safe over there, and don't forget you will be deeply miss by me, I don't regret what we did, infidelity or not, I love you a lot, and that the truth." I looked into her eyes and replied, "Thank you, I'm miss you too." Ms. President herself, Ulrica, came up to me, after Marcie walked away with hugging arms and kissing lips replying, "This is a very significant visit, you are about to make for members of yours ethnicity, take care of yourself, I'm sending a group of Secret Service men with you, just in case some foul play occurs over there, and don't forget you have a wife and three children, praying for you to return home save, I do love you, first gentleman Bobby Wilson."

I felt as though, I was in the military again, leaving home on active duty to serve my country overseas for some type of secret political purpose, after boarding my flight, I look back, and saw the leader of this nation, wiping tears from her eyes with a firm smile on her face.

The flight to Africa was a memorable one on a Concord Jet Liner from the J.F.K. Airport in New York to Paris, France, and from Paris to Algiers, Algeria. Where Ulrica's half-brother Johnny and his lovely wife, Natasha, greeted me. I was invited by them to go on a six months political tour with them, visiting different Africa's nations promoting a political alliance among them.

I was taken to a hotel, where I would be staying, during my visit to Algeria. Johnny and Natasha invited me to their home, but I turned down their hospitality. I wanted to be free among the people of Algeria to enhance my writing experience. I met a group of people at the hotel, where I was staying known as the A.A.A.O. African Alliance Associating Organization.

There were one hundred members, tell people representing each of the ten Africa's nations attending: Algeria, Angola, Congo, Egypt, Ethiopia, Libya, Nigeria, South Africa, South-West Africa and Zaire. I noticed that all Africans weren't black or dark-complexioned people, seen as though some Caucasian from Europe have blended their blood to create different shades of colors to the Africans world, but these members of the A.A.A.O. are determine to modernize the continent of Africa as a world leader in civilization, technology, medicine, agriculture, scientific inventions, education, military strength and humanitarian.

These countries have some of their brightest students serving as exchange students, studying at some of the great universities in Asia, Europe and America to enhance their knowledge as intellectual scholars, returning home to teach their people what they have learned. Higher education and hospitalization were free to the citizen of these countries.

Their political systems were becoming more interest in democracy with moderating ingredient. Their governing officials provide their citizens with the necessary means to obtain a decent lifestyle, and in return these citizens serve their countries with the contributions to support other citizen in need.

I received the escort of a beautiful French-Algerian lady by the name of Bianca. She's a political activist appointed by Natasha to make sure my stay in Algiers was a pleasant and memorable one, touring and enjoying the lifestyle of the affluent Algerians. She was all the comfort a man needed about a woman. We discussed different topics of life in the U.S. during dinner, and she gained some important insights, from me expressing my opinions, concerning the enhancement of her country.

I also met some powerful people, while visiting different areas of Algeria, including the natives and wild life. When it was time for me to move on to Tripoli, as a farewell gift, Blanca intellectually seduced me into an intimate bliss, sexually this lady was well equipped. While sexually indulging with her, I had no thought of infidelity. I felt like she was rewarding me for doing an impressive job, and to encounter such a clandestine affair, which was instigated by her, for me to participate in this orgasm-causing ordeal, was an obligation for me, to make love to such a beautiful lady. While leaving Algeria, I closed my eyes, visualizing her salacious nude body, copulating with mine, having a sexual good time.

My two weeks visit to Libya was somewhat of a political secret, because this country and the United States weren't getting along with each other, and there was another princess there to greet me, a Libyan lady with political ties to the A.A.A.O. She was to be my escort, during my stay there, and her name was Almira. She was hired to portray the role of my wife. Her concern was to change the political role of Libya's leaders.

We were together, at a party given by Libya's President, at his palace in the Capitol City of Tripoli, mingling with affluent as well as influential guests. Almira was serving as my interpreter, to make sure I understood, what was being said to me, and my reply would be just as appropriated to my listeners. She stood by my side at all times with a bright friendly smile on her face. Of all the Libyan women, I had seen during my visit, Almira was more eyes pleasing to see, with a stimulating body figure, seducing me intellectually.

At the moment, we were really enjoying ourselves with the guests; there was a military-coup invasion against the leader of Libya, at this party. People were rushing into the Capitol's palace armed with automatic weapons, shooting their guns, and launching grenades into the crowd of partying people. Bullets were ripping through their bodies, grenades were exploding, blowing people to pieces, flesh and blood splashed against Almira and my bodies and faces, as we were blown to the floor by the grenades blasts.

Almira tackled me on the floor, shielding my body with hers, telling me to crawl to the hallway. She was running, while leading me by the hand, and some of the gunmen, started shooting at us, bullets bouncing off the wall, that when I took the lead, running with Almira's hand in mine. I was almost dragging her, because she wasn't running fast enough to keep up with me, then she shouted out to me, "Bobby, jump down the linen tunnel!" I dove into the linen tunnel with Almira behind me. We slid three stories down the tunnel, out of it into a linen basket with enough force to cause the basket to roll away from the tunnel, lucky for us, because soon after that, a grenade fell out of the tunnel and exploded. The force from the grenade's explosion pushed the basket faster down the hall.

At that time, a group of American men, appealed to be members of the C.I.A. surrounded us with military weapons, firing at the invaders, while Almira led me into an armor tank. There inside the tank, we got undressed; her body was looking great, as she took the bloody clothes off, dressed only in her panties and bra. I was too scared to get an erection, and then we dressed ourselves, in bulletproof clothing, from our heads to our toes.

Almira gave me an automatic rifle replying, "I hope you haven't lost your marksmanship, because we are in a do or die situation here." All of a sudden the tank stopped, she and I jumped out, shooting our guns, running for cover, behind buildings and ducking through alleys.

Almira led me to a jeep parked, with a driver in it, waiting at the end of the alley. We got into the jeep, and were taken out of town. There while traveling up and down hills in this desert, Almira received some information on her headset. She quickly shouted, while jumping out of the moving jeep, snatching me with her. "Jump! We're under an attack." We fell to the ground, rolling down the sandy hill, seconds later a rocket hit the jeep, and blew it to pieces.

When Almira and I reached the bottom of the hill, a caravan of Camels was passing through, and we became passengers on a Camel's back, all the way to the coast line. Almira found a way for her and me to become store-a- way in the bottom of a cargo ship heading for Ababa, Ethiopia. We were in a space that store sheep's wool. While lying on the pile of wool, I was exhausted and frightened, until I felt asleep, after feeling the sting of a needle, injecting something into my arm.

There I began to dream about Almira and me making passionate love. I also witnessed the thrill of an orgasm during this dream. When

I awakened, I found myself nude, lying on my back wet with sweat, and Almira's sweaty wet nude body was lying on top of me. She was sound asleep, that's when I realized I wasn't dreaming at all. Almira had injected some type of drug into my arm to sedate me, and she seduced me into having sex with her, and our physical performance was like a dream.

The drug, she had injected into my body made me sleepy and horny, also caused me to witness some moments of amnesia. I didn't remember getting undress, all of this was a dream to me, but when I awaken, and saw her salaciously nude body, lying on top of me, I received another erection, and wanted to do it again, she accommodated me. There's nothing like having sex with a woman, who processes a warm, wet and fitting vagina. I thought, I would never see my wife and family again, and under this type of situation, if sex was available, may as well indulge while I'm able.

Almira had a bag of clothes for us to wear. We dressed like the crews of this cargo ship. For a few days, we stay down in the cargo space, eating different kinds of fruits for our meal. Almira and I discussed the political changes; she planned on discussing with the new leader of Libya. She was an entrepreneur, living a lucrative lifestyle, with the inclination to contribute to the political changes of her country, and made the initiative to be my escort for the United States support in her endeavor.

After a few days of living below deck in this cargo space, Almira got bold, and suggested that we should go to the mess deck and have chow with the rest of the crews, and we did just that, without being too much notice. We ate a decent meal. There while eating, Almira over heard some of the crew talking about the leader of Libya was overthrown.

Almira went to the captain of this ship, and began to talk with him, after the conversation, Almira and I were assigned to a state room of this ship, as the captain's guest, and we enjoyed his hospitality all the way to the port of Ethiopia, where Johnny and Natasha were there to greet us with detail of my next mission.

Almira and I had our final dinner together at that hotel, and we managed to find a secluded place, to say out farewell to each other with hugs and kisses, afterward Almira expressed her appreciation to me, for being there with her during that hostile situation, and she also apologize for putting my life in danger, before whispering these words into my ear. "Our intimate rendezvous in the cargo space of that ship will be a charitable memory, of our clandestine ordeal, to forget it, I never will."

Johnny had set up a televised conversation between my wife, the president of the United States and me. Only her face was seen, while we talked to each other through this television screen. Ulrica apologized to me for almost losing my life, and I asked her why she wanted to jeopardize my life like that anyway, and she replied, "For the sake of your ethnicity, your signature will guarantee that the United States will assist these countries of Africa in gaining world power and recognition.

"Most of my security people who started this trip with you, men and women are not living. They were killed in the coup attempt in Libya." Ulrica assured me that my new security force would consist of a group of military elite, representing each branch of the United States military. I saw and spoke to each of my children through this televised communication equipment, Ulrica and Johnny had collaborated on setting up this communication, so no one else could hear or see us.

Bobby J., Victoria and Little Edmond were there, looking great, smiling, glad to hear and see their daddy again, asking me, when I'm coming home. Ulrica interrupting them, saying that I will be home in three more months, before telling me that the news medias had printed rumors that I was dead or missing, during the coup attempt, which ended up a success, because they did kill the president of Libya.

I asked Ulrica why the first man of the United States had to go on such a life-threatening mission. She replied, "I thought, I had answered that question before, you were requested by these countries, and your mission there is significant, for those people of your ethnicity, to achieve world recognition, in different ways of competing in modernizing their political, economic, technology and natural resources, and since I'm proclaimed to be a domestic president, and implementing solutions for different issues of this country.

"You will be honored by these people, when your mission is finished, and clandestinely speaking, don't let your infidelity attitude, causes you to lose a beautiful and powerful wife, and the children of your life. I would let you talk to Marcie, but she's not with us anymore, she decided to resign from being our nanny, because she got pregnant by Pedro. They decided to get marry and move to Mexico."

My mission with the A.A.A.O. nations of Africa alliance was restricted to international business with Ethiopia, Egypt, Congo, Nigeria, South Africa, South-West Africa and Zaire. My signature enabled the United States to exchange goods with these African nations. They brought more of American technology to become self-sufficient in utilizing their natural resource to profit affluently from other countries doing business with them, and to buy what they need, to enhance their existences, especially with agriculture improving their irrigation systems, growing crops where they never grown before, increasing the number of livestock in each of these countries, also modernizing places of residents, transportations, and military weapons.

By utilizing their natural resource, to make the type of money, they need to buy more medical technologies, communication equipments, and educational enhancement, finally there was a cure for AIDS, discovered by the collaboration of each nation's scientists, as well as the secret knowledge of how the virus of AIDS got to Africa, and how such epidemic spread so rapidly, killing millions of people, because of their immune systems couldn't resist this deadly virus.

A secret rumor occurred that there was a place in Iceland, where no black person had ever lived. They built an under ice covered ground laboratory there, producing such a deadly disease, trying to commit genocide against the African people. They were clandestinely spraying this deadly virus across the skies of Africa, but to the creator of this virus surprise, his scheme somehow backfired. This disease-causing virus was killing people of other ethnicities too, but not nearly as many as the African people. So this racial conspiracy, clandestinely continued, until a group of scientists from these powerful African nations, began to collaborate their strategies diligently enough, until they found a cure for the disease that was killing millions of their people.

My touring mission throughout these African nations was over with, although, I enjoyed my signature visit to the mother's land, I was glad as hell, heading back to the United States. I wanted to kiss the ground, and yes, I accomplished what was required of me, except for the leisure time, I once had with the African women had ceased, under the direct order of my wife, the United States President, having members of her elite security force watching me close.

I was there strictly on business, listening to lectures from their leaders, and expressing my opinions about the situations, they were trying to implement, as a collaborating groups of African nations, and my signature on certain documents guaranteed them aid from the United States, as a fair trade proposition for some of their natural resources, that will benefit us.

When I arrived at the airport of Washington, D.C., I was greeted by my family, I was glad and surprise to see my pregnant wife, presiding over this great nation of our, and my three children with hugs and kisses dearly. Ulrica had accomplished in nine months, more than some of the formal presidents did in years. For instant, she was implementing a plan to give African- American citizens, who can prove that their ancestors, as family members, were slaves in the United States, and promised forty acres of land and a mule, will receive what was promised to their ancestors.

Ulrica offered them forty acres of land with a vehicle, if they accept the land in either of these states: Nebraska, Utah, Wyoming, North Dakota, South Dakota, Iowa, Montana or Idaho. This was an effort to relocate some of the black citizens from the southern ghettoes into these areas of diversity, and an effort to cut down, black on black crimes, but some of those Negroes refused to go, complaining about those states get too cold in the winter time, but with the incentive of a business and home grant or loan, some black citizens with a large numbers of family members, took interest in this proposition, to relocate from the heavy population of blacks, in those southern states to those states, that were lacking a sufficient number of black citizens. This was the president's way of spreading equality throughout the United States.

I returned home, from a six months long mission, of negotiating ways to enhance, the existence of my ethnicity in Africa. While my wife the President of the United States was trying her best to undo the curse that the administration of the first president of this nation, placed on black people by forcing them into slavery a crime against humanity, was her way to alleviate racial discrimination.

I don't know why Ulrica was executing so well as the Commander In Chief of this nation, The United States, but most of the other politicians are negotiating with her proposition in a compromising way. Maybe it's because, she was pregnant, and presiding with a mother figure over this nation, showing her concern for all citizen, dealing with the issues of their interests, separate and collectively.

Ulrica was off in her ninth month of pregnancy, and I hadn't been with my family for a while. I play and show love to my three children, until they fell asleep on top of me. After our new nanny had put them to bed, an elderly Caucasian lady known as Mrs. Smith.

While Ulrica and I were in the master bedroom of the White House, something about the word master, I didn't appreciate. I had taken a shower, ready for bed. Ulrica was there in front of her dresser's mirror, lotioning herself, everything about my wife's body was still eye pleasing to see stimulatingly, except her swollen stomach, it just didn't look seductive to me. I questioned her decision of not telling me that she was pregnant. She said, she wanted it to be a surprise, and I responded, "I been gone away from home, six months long, and when I return, I can't make love to my wife, because she is in her ninth and final month of pregnancy."

Ulrica spoke in a sarcastic way. "Well, I would apologize for my condition, but you are at fault of it, by fertilizing me, each time we indulge intimately, while I'm ovulating, and this is the last baby, I'm giving birth to, you hear me, too bad Marcie is not here, I'm sure you won't object, she clandestinely substitute for me, as a surrogate for my husband and children."

I replied quickly, "She was our nanny, doing the job, you sometime avoided, because of your political interest. Why did you marry me anyway? If it was love, well, I'm damn sure not getting my portion of it, by being the husband of the United States President. I may as well be impotent, you are trying to solve the problems of this country's citizens, and neglecting my intimate need."

Ulrica stared at me with tears in her eyes, and then she gave me a sexy smile, apologizing to me with hugs and kisses, stimulating me with her fellatio technique, before whispering these words into my ear. "I'm tell you what, I'm going to do, I'm let you ease into my backdoor, but you must promise to do it nice and slow. You are my husband, and I love you so much, sometime it hurts, to think of us breaking up."

We were careful about making love under her condition. I was so horny. I just had to ease into her warm wet stretching to fit pregnant vagina. Everything was so lovely and nice; it felt like paradise, making good warm passionate love, to my willing wife, in the master bedroom of the White House. Just as I, began to experience the thrill of life, gritting my teeth and closing my eyes, moaning out loud, Ulrica went into labor, she began to give birth to our baby, as we lay.

I thought she was going insane, when she groaned out these words. "I want to give natural birth to our little girl, and name her after your deceased mother, Shuler Denise Wilson. Oh baby, put some rubbing alcohol on your hands, come on let's do this together." You talking about somebody becoming a nervous fellow in a hurry, I was shaking and trembling uncontrollably. Ulrica lay on her back in the bed, raising her legs at knee level, and spreading them, while I was in the bathroom, trying to disinfect my hands with rubbing alcohol.

Ulrica screamed out loud, and I ran to her, just as our baby girl was being pushed out of her mother into this world. I was there to gently pull this little girl on into this world, and she began to cry like she was fussing. The security people were alarmed by Ulrica's scream, and they rushed into our bedroom in a hurry. They saw me taking my daughter from her mother's body, and placing her on Ulrica's stomach. Her navel cord was still attached to her mother.

The female security people ran to assist me, while the security men made a quick about face, running outside the bedroom to get medical assistant, and they showed up within minutes, rushing to do, what it takes, to make sure the President of the United States was okay. Ulrica with me and little Shuler D. was taken to the hospital quickly, making head line news, throughout to news medias. "President Ulrica D'Angelo-Wilson gave natural birth last night to her fourth child and second daughter, with her husband, the First Gentleman Bobby Wilson, there assisting her, who had clandestinely returned to the United States, from his six months mission in Africa.

"What a terrific timing for Mrs. President, to deliver her baby on the night of the day, her husband returned to the United States. She gave birth to a cute and healthy, seven pounds baby girl, name after the first gentleman's deceased mother, Shuler Denise Wilson. The President is resting peaceful in the hospital, and will return to the white house in a day or two, for little Shuler D. to meet the rest of her siblings."

Ulrica didn't waste any time, getting her body back into shape, the way I appreciated it. We were doing calisthenics just about every day, until her stomach was flat and stimulating. The majority of the citizens of this country seen to admire my wife, their president's intellectual attractiveness, dressed in the expensive clothes, that she wore, as a domestic president, focusing on solving problems at home, foreign affair wasn't too much of her interest. She wanted all U.S. citizens to be treated equally and decent with respect from the politicians.

Ulrica had implemented a law to prevent businesses and other institutions from charging consumers added fee and sub payments, and to enhance the relationship between businesses and consumers, just as consumers were charged with criminal offense for shop lifting or taking merchandises from these businesses without paying for them, business people could also face criminal charges for overcharging the consumers or selling them improper products or services.

Ulrica was also pushing a tougher law for a cleaner environment; the water and air need to be taken care for the longevity of human existences. Polluters, if find guilty can face a heavy fine or do some jail time. Federal money was being spent to clean up rivers, lakes, ponds and screams. Oil and other manufacturing industries were being charged to keep the air clean. Wild life habitat was being reserved. Forests were being more protected. It was mandatory for lumbers companies to replant trees, as they remove them.

Racism was a crime punished by law. If anyone was accused of racially insulting another person, he or she can be convicted to do time in jail or prison. It was mandatory that members of each major ethnicity be represented in the occupational fields, social organizations or any event where people gather to socialize, and multicultural became a national holiday. People of different ethnicities would get together, and celebrate such diversity, becoming more familiar with the different lives styles migrated into this great nation.

The welfare system required on the job training for the recipients, birth control was free, and mandatory for girls at their adolescent stages to take, when they began to date, and woman's choice was a law. College education was also mandatory; public schools were free, until the students received a Bachelor degree. Federal taxes were exempted from citizen, who were earning less the twenty thousand a year, and minimum wages were raised to ten dollars an hour.

People earning between twenty-five and thirty five thousand dollars yearly, pay five per cent of their annual earning to federal income taxes. The more money each citizen makes, the more taxes they would have to pay, especially those who make sixty thousand dollars or more. Ulrica thought this tax scenario would give the common people a fair chance to live more decent. As the United States President, Ulrica wanted more quality military personnel, so the military draft system, was once again implemented, to get these types of people into the military, with free college education for military   personnel,   their   spouses, and   dependents.   Military   personnel stationed overseas were exempted from federal income taxes while out of the country.

Ulrica presided over this country the way she governed the state of Oregon, making the United States a great place to live without racism being an issue. People who moved their businesses to foreign countries lose their citizenship here.

Six months, after I had returned to the United States, there was a huge mushroom type of explosion in the North Pole, against Iceland's underground laboratory. This lab was clandestinely bombed, no one took credit for doing it or was accused of doing it, but it happened to this lab, where they suspected there was some type of virus secretly being created to kill off black people.

Now the result of such explosion, turning the mushroom cloud into a mysterious mist, blowing across the globe, if this mist was breathed in by albino type of Caucasian women or those type of women with very light or pale complexions, this mist consisted of a disease causing virus, affecting the reproduction system, of these women in a deadly way, causing them to die from such illness, and the numbers of their death were on the increase with no cure for it.

It started off with those types of Scandinavian women living in Norway, Sweden, Denmark, Greenland, Finland and Iceland, then this disease spread throughout Europe, Canada and Australia. These women were dying by the millions within a year. Such a disease, also begin to affect the very pale complexioned women in Asia, and other places of this world, until a scientist from South Africa discovered a cure for such deadly illness affecting these types of women throughout the world.

This cure was televised live throughout the world. This South Africa Scientist, Dr. Mendoza was parented by a black South Africa man, and an English borne Caucasian woman, he was experimenting with some of the women with this rare and deadly disease with pure blooded black complexioned African men, and this experimentation caused for sexual indulgent between these dying Caucasian ladies and African men.

If these ladies become pregnant, and during their nine months of pregnancy, this deadly disease began to cease, subsiding during the duration of their pregnancy, while their reproduction system got stronger, and after they gave birth to their biracial babies, there was no sign of this deadly disease, affecting these types of women's reproductive systems again. They were completely cure of this ethnical disease, and their new borne were healthy and strong.

This was a worldwide alert for white women dying under this condition. Most of them began to seek black men as their lovers, husbands or babies making surrogates, to keep them from going under, to the cause of death, and there was a conflict of interest when these European women, and other women of this world were dying in a hurry, seeking refuge of this deadly disease, with the intimacy pure black complexioned men had to give them.

A mass numbers of these Caucasian women went to Africa to become residents, seeking to have sex with the native men of this continent in order to get pregnant, the only way to cure them of this deadly disease. Some of these women were married, and became victims of homicide, because their husbands rather for them to die, before accepting the fact that black men will have to lay between their wives' white thighs, to produce a child to save their lives. Some of these women were forced to commit suicide by their husbands, and others women filed for divorces, and let the world know, about the condition they were in.

Most of these European women migrated to Africa to save their lives by giving birth to a biracial child, and some of them were rich enough to take their African husbands or lovers back to the land, they were borne and loved.

The Asian women who were suffering under this same deadly disease went to India to mate with their original black men, setting up residents there or taking their mates back to the country where they lived, and a lot of Canadian women found a political way to mate with the black complexioned men of the United States, and some of them explored the prisons system of the United States, just to get pregnant by certain black inmates.

Some of these inmates who were serving time under good behaviors, were rehabilitated to marry these ladies, who returned to Canada with their husbands and pregnant with biracial babies. There also were some light complexioned Caucasian American women dying under this same condition, but not as many as those women from other countries, and they too explored southern states of the United States, seeking out to find pure black blooded men to mate with them, so that they may continue to live.

The Australia women who were dying from this deadly disease began to mate with their aboriginal natives of that continent or the Nigritoes of the Philippine Islands. Scientists predicted within four years, a fourth of the world population will be people of biracial characteristic, that when the Caucasian scientists got hard to work, collaborating on a cure for these ladies, without them having babies by black men.

African nations became stiff competitions in the world summer Olympic games, and as a whole they won more gold medals, than any other countries participating in these sporting events, except for the United States. The American black athletes had to put forward their American pride, to motivate their efforts to win over their African competitors, and a lot of those athletes representing different African nations had Caucasian wives from different countries of Europe, cheering their husbands on to victory.

European scientists were working diligently on their research, trying to find a cure for this mysterious deadly disease that was only affecting those very pale complexioned Caucasian women of Europe, Canada, Australia, Asian, New Zealand and American women with this type of complexion, were suffering from this type of illness, and to make babies with black complexioned men, causing interracial relationship to increase between black men and white women, until miraculously a pill was invented to take the place of black men and white women babies making technique. What a release for the black women and white men with ethnocentric attitudes.

By the time this pill was distributed worldwide, one fourth of Europe population was African related, mixing their blood and culture with Caucasian women. The Caucasian men of Europe became jealous with hatred attitudes toward the African natives, even though there was a pill to cure this disease, affecting white women's reproductive systems. The younger generation of Caucasian women took a liking toward black men, because they see to product better looking and healthy babies with these types of Caucasian ladies.

The European Caucasian men started a conflict with the African men living in their countries, by organizing hate groups, who clandestinely started to burn them out, taking some of their lives, expediting them back to Africa without their families and wives, causing a war between Africa and Europe to break out. The United States remained neutral, taking no side, serving as a mediator, trying to get these countries of black and white pride to negotiate in a compromising way, working on a resolution to a peaceful conclusion.

The United States threat to intervene only if either side try to use nuclear weapons or weapon of mass destruction on each other. President Ulrica D'Angelo Wilson had the United States military forces on fully alert around the globe. She refused to visit any country at war with each other. The President's yacht was named First Navy. It was a big luxury ship equipped with military weapons to protect the Commander In Chief, surrounded by the seventh or sixth fleet, depending on where she decided to meet leaders of different countries in international water, trying to reach a peaceful agreement between these countries at war with each other's.

Within six months of the Africa and Europe military conflict, a similar situation occurred between Asia and India, invading each other land with military equipments. The Hinduisms of India declared war against the Buddhists of China, Japan and other Asian countries, then Australia found faults with New Zealand's political process, and they decided to take military action against each other. Just as the United States had implemented, the initiative of adding Cuba and Jamaica as states to this nation, since Cuba had embraced democracy, and expelled their dictation ship, and began to vote to elect their governing officials, and Jamaica requested statement ship to the United States. These two states situations were put on hold, until a future date.

South America had instigated a conflict with the countries of the Middle East which caused for military invasion on both sides, and terrorism let their presence be known using human as bombs.

Canada became an ally of Australia against New Zealand. Afghanistan and Pakistan became allies of New Zealand. Seen like the world was bloodthirsty to kill up each other, and the United States military was at full force around the globe, trying to negotiate a peaceful solution between these countries, trying to annihilate one another.

There were citizens of the United States clandestinely giving up their citizenship, just to go and fight for the countries representing their ethnicities. Blacks, Whites, Asian and Hispanic-American people took interest in this World War III event. The United States was the only peaceful place to live, until Europe try to clandestinely launch a nuclear attack on those African nations fighting so diligently, and Europe wanted to eliminate their persistence to win this military conflict between the two continents.

The action Europe was about to take against these fighting African nations caused the United States to intervene with their satellite nuclear weapons disarmament laser defense system, shutting down Europe capability to launch a nuclear attack against Africa, who was really to retaliate, and the result of this nuclear hush by the United States, let Europe and the rest of the world know, that this country was capable of defeating any and all countries of this world, with nuclear weapon capabilities, and the result of this show of power, by the United States had all of the fighting countries, with nuclear weapons capability, leaders coming back to the negotiating table, to discuss a peaceful solution for humanity sake, before the United States force them to have it her way, and all of the invading militaries forces began to pull out of their enemies territories.

As World War III began to end, and seek peace with their enemies, there was a law passed in the United States against obesity, claiming that these types of people were consuming too much food, and during the time, the world was at war, there was a food shortage. Some of the thinner people and politicians were claiming that obesity is really not an illness, it's just that these people are greedy and love to eat, abusing food, until they become corpulent in their appearances, proposing a law against those rude people abusing food, because they love to eat.

The military has a law against obesity. Why not civilian lawmakers do the same? Make it a law against people over eating. This legal action caused fat people to take their grief to the streets, protesting a march in Washington, D.C. It was fearful to see such a mass numbers of large size people of different ethnicities, gender, sexualities and belief, protesting against a law passed to control their eating habit.

These people of obesity were given the ultimatum of losing weight, at a certain time or go to jail, where there was a special facility, to house people of obese, to stay on a program utilizing certain vitamins and nutrient supplements for them to take with just water to drink, and a small amount of bread to eat. This made the people of obesity angry and they took their frustrations to the streets of Washington, D.C.

I have never in my life; seen so many large size people in one place, and their angry appearances were intimidating to see. They were there tall in height and large in size, short in height and large in size, also medium in height and large in size. They were blacks, whites, Asians and Hispanic people, there protesting this law, trying to control how much they should eat. People of different religions, classes of living, men and women, girls and boys, homosexual and heterosexual people there representing their eating condition.

Just as President D'Angelo-Wilson found a solution to end World War Three, by bringing peace to those fighting countries around the world. No one expected such a domestic problem as this, and of all the countries of this world, the United States was leading the world with a growing number of obesity, and to control such an illness, congress passed a law against people over eating, which frustrated a whole lots of overweighed American citizens, who took to the streets of Washington, D.C., marching to the lawn of the White House, where the Speaker of the House came out to discuss this law with them.

Before the Speaker of the House, Mr. Donald Nelson could quiet these fat angry people down to listen to him, here comes a group of small and slim people, marching to counteract a protest against these fat people, and that when a riot broke out, big and little people fighting each other's in the streets of Washington, D.C. Those big people were physically getting the best of these little people, until more and more little and regular size people got involved in the nationwide brawl between obese and small or regular size people.

This incident turned spouse against each other, husbands and wives were fighting on different side, same as for sisters and brothers, nieces, nephews and cousins were in the streets fighting each other, because of the size of each individual. People were being hospitalized. Some of them die from being physically brutalized. Blood was spilled in the streets of Washington, D.C. There weren't enough policemen to control this catastrophe.

I thought it would be a race war or a war between sexualities, erupting throughout the United States, never would I have dreamed that such a situation as this, people of different sizes fighting in the streets of Washington, D.C., because a law was passed against obesity. Cars, trucks and buses were being turned over, bombed and burned, homes and businesses, being damaged by these people rioting in the streets.

The National Guard was called out to restore order, and there was a curfew placed throughout the United States, because people of different size nationwide declared war on each other in every state. This incident even had children fighting each other in schools. Since this was a nationwide size war going on throughout this country, Ulrica felt it was her presidential duty to find a solution to stop this confusion between obese and regular size people.

She called for a conference meeting with the leaders, representing each side of this nationwide conflict, asking them to put an end to this chaos, after negotiating with each other, compromising on a solution, putting an end to this conflict between the size of people, by deleting the law that was written against obesity, because there was a lunatic holding a fatal grudge against fat people, and became a series killer against obesity.

He was driving from state to state in a van with three Pit Bull dogs, a change saw and a can of gasoline, killing his victims by letting his dogs attack them, mauling them to death, leaving their corpses lying there or he would sneak up on his victims with a change saw, and cut their bodies to pieces. He was having fun committing such hideous crime, chasing some of his victims down, splashing gasoline on their bodies, burning them alive, driving away laughing.

He would even video each of his killing, but he got caught in the state of Arkansas, the police arrived on the scene of his dogs attacking a fat female human being. The dogs were shot to death, and he was arrested, trying to claim his innocence by insanity.

This series killer name was Frank Sherman, a resident of Florida state, who was once in the United States Navy, stationed abroad a ship, that took a six month cruise overseas, confessing that when he left the United States with the navy, his wife had a cute face, with eyes pleasing to see, salacious body figure, and within six month, she went on an eating spree, turning a fine lovely lady into a fat ugly woman.

When Frank returned home, it hurt his feeling to see his wife in this condition, three time the size she was, before he left the United States with the navy, and they started an altercation, he was calling her obscene names, and she retaliated, when he slapped her face, calling her a big fat Collins green eating bitch.

She grabbed him in a bear hug, and throws his body into the wall, snatching him from the wall. He was too hurt to defend himself from her, and she throw him through their glass door, before calling the police, and he was arrested for domestic violent, physically abusing his wife. She pressed charges against him, and he was arrested and went to jail.

After he was released from jail, he clandestinely killed his wife, and went on a killing spree, taking his grudge out on all fat people, men and women. He had killed seventeen innocent people, before he got caught, claiming their obese appearances offended him, hurting his feeling, because they were fat ugly human beings, eyes sore to see, and the jury of his peer didn't hesitate about giving him the death penalty.

There was an assassinating attempt on my life inside the White House by a Secret Service lady, while I was in bed with my wife the president having sex play, and it went this way. Ulrica and I had just finished taking a relaxing bath together. I had my bathrobe on, walking around the bedroom, sipping on a stimulating drink, while observing my wife, putting lotion on her body.

I started joking with her about me being so rich, I could feces on the White House's floor, and look the president in the face, and said clean it up. Ulrica replied with a smile on her face, "Oh, I remember reading something like that from your junk manuscript, yes as I recalled, it went something like this, you looked the president in the face, and said clean it up whore, yeah you just talked yourself out of some loving tonight."

I replied, "I apologize, don't make me turn into a Vampire Werewolf, and eat you alive." I usually play with my wife this way, so I started crawling up on her, tenderly biting the flesh of her toes, and Ulrica began to laugh while portraying her role as the victim, backing up on the bed as though she was scare. I began to growl like a wild animal, biting the flesh of her legs in a stimulating way, and she said in a frightful way, "Ah, this feels great."

I continue to crawl up on her body, until I was lying between her legs, while biting against the fresh of her neck, as if I was a Vampire, and she let out a loud stimulating scream, forgetting she was the president of the United States. "Oh, you are killing me!" All of a sudden our bedroom's door flew open, and Secret Service people came rushing into our bedroom with their weapons drawn, pointing at me. Ulrica rolled her body on top of mine replying, "Holster those damn weapons, now! And get the hell out of my bedroom."

This particular Caucasian Secret Service lady had run on the other side of the bed, aiming to shoot me dead, while I was laying under Ulrica. I closed my eyes, and heard two shots fired. I didn't feel any pain, as I heard someone fall to the floor. When I opened my eyes, Ulrica had reached behind the mattress of our bed, and pulled out her three eighty automatic pistol, and shot this Secret Service lady. Who was hired to assassinate me, but Ulrica reacted too quickly interfered with her assassinating attempt.

This Secret Service lady was rushed to the hospital where she dies, and there was an investigation on this lady. Melissa Halter was her name, an ex- marine with military fame, who also was a part of the coup attack in Libya, attempting to kill me there, but she missed, and somehow she was substituting in the place of a regular Secret Service agent, who was on emergency leave, giving her a second to kill me, but my wife shot her down in the White House.

The news medias instigated this incident in an incredible way, making the President of the United States a hero. The first female president of the United States, Ms. Ulrica D'Angelo-Wilson, had to take the life of a Secret Service agent, in order to save the life of her spouse. The citizens of this country were proud of this presiding woman, knowing now that she has what it takes to be The Commander In Chief of this great nation, and a bulletproof vest, became a part of my everyday attire.

This world will never be a perfect place to live as long as the individuality of people is represented mental, emotional and physically, because some people focus on their mental existences, to be knowledgeable and ingenious, but lacking the concern of their fellow human beings, while those focusing on their emotional interests, showing humanitarian concern for the less fortunate people, suffering from malnutrition, destitute, lack of proper medicine, and shelters, offering their monetary assistant to better the lives of these unfortunate citizens living conditions; whereas those people with physical concern, keeping their bodies in shape in a healthy way, caring less about other people maintaining physical strength.

Those human beings having a balanced concern about their mental, emotional and physical state of existences as total individuals are the ones in competition with each other, trying to be better than the next person. These are the type of people who will trouble the world of one another, causing conflict of interest to exist among this world of people, because they are conceited, and rather fight than to take someone's advice or to give into other people decisions, bring about the meaning of debate and altercation, can't negotiate in a compromising way, because their attitudes get in the way, causing a conflict to evolve during the situation.

Disaster Sunday

This was the Sunday during professional football play off-season; every stadium of the United States had a record-breaking number of fans there, cheering for their team to win the game. President D'Angelo-Wilson, and the first family decided to take a break from Washington, D.C., to spend some time on their ranch in Oregon.

This particular football Sunday, I was watching the game on television, so I could be around my family members. It's amazing how time flies, Bobby J. and Victoria were big size children in grade school, private of course, vacationing at the ranch with us, little Edmond running around the house making noise, and cute little Shuler, the most beautiful baby alive, laid in my arms so cuddly sweet, until she felt asleep, and here come her mother Ulrica, taking her away from me, and putting her in bed. It was nice being alone with my family members, and not a group of political people always around, trying to lobby for this and that.

I was sitting in my comfortable chair, drinking on a glass of beer. Ulrica was experiencing her monthly P.M.S. (premenstrual syndrome) mood, showing me a rude attitude, but with the children, she is a fun having mama, showing them love and comfort. The game on television was getting, exciting to see, watching my favorite team's player return a kick off run all the way back for a touchdown. He was breaking away from tacklers, faking out other players, causing them to miss their tackle on him. I was standing up out of my seat, cheering out loud, when I heard Ulrica complaining. "Bobby, you are too loud, don't forget Shuler D. is asleep, if you wait her up, she is going to be crying loud like she's fussing."

Then all of a sudden, four bright lights came falling from the sky, on television, they looked like shooting or falling stars, each hitting a fourth section of the stadium consecutively, exploring with a monstrous sound of thunders rolling into one huge mushroom ball of fire and smoke, going upward beyond the cloud, leaving nothing but a huge hole in the ground, where the stadium once stood seconds ago. Everything went up in fame, the structure of the stadium, and all the thousands of its spectators went up into this huge mushroom of fire and smoke, cremating all the people it consumed with this stadium, and their ashes were a part of the fallout from the mushroom cloud, as it dissipated, evaporating into the atmosphere.

Each professional football stadium with a game being played in that Sunday was attacked the same way, causing some of the elder people, viewing their televisions to die from heart attacks, caused by the shocks they received from what they saw on T.V. Ulrica received a red telephone call with alert D in process, and she gave direct order to retaliate on every country with nuclear capability.

The attack was on, but at that time little did the United States knew, that every country around the world with a large crowd of people in their arenas, was attacked the same way, with what appeared to be falling stars, exploring upon impact like miniatures nuclear bombs. The United States disarmed every country with nuclear weapons, and forced them to surrender under the authority of the United States Democracy, putting an end to the nobility of Kings and Queens. U.S. ranking military officials were placed in charge of those countries we had conquered.

As the U.S. military was utilizing strategy to find out who almost demolished the existence of American citizens, executive order from the President of the United States, that all television stations stop televising this shocking catastrophe, that almost wipe out the middle and some upper class people, most of those in their prime age of living, and love to attend football events, each stadium was occupied by the majority of these people, and there were only a few corpses to be buried, also a few people survived this deadly attack on American favorite sport activity.

Some of the people on the playing field were injured, due to the fact that those explosions went from the ground upward, deafening those from the sound of the blasts, and binding them with the bright flash. President Ulrica D'Angelo-Wilson, with her family and administrative staff were rush to an underground palace, somewhere in the state of Kansas, where they were debating that the new White House with black trimming should be built. President D'Angelo-Wilson was putting forward diligent effort to assure the American people, with confident that this is not the end of the world, just an inevitable situation, and it will be taken care of.

The world had a stale smell in the air, and this mysterious disaster left the president with the decision of moving people from the ghettoes, and other low class living areas of this country into places, where those who lose their lives by these deadly explosions once lived, and no one knew where those deadly explosions came from, they were seen falling from the sky, in broad daylight.

A lot of Caucasian people die on that day, because the majority of the people in those football stadiums on disaster Sunday were Caucasians. The counts of the decease or those people missing were in the millions, lowering the ratio of black and white citizens.

People were being released from jail and prison under good condition to reestablish the American dream. Young people during their adolescent stage of life were encourage to get marry, and produce a family to increase the population of this country, and the properties of those citizen who lost their lives in this great tragedy, and there was no family members to claim them, were given to the less fortunate citizens.

Countries around the world were pointing their fingers at one another, accusing each other for their troubles. The United States had such an inevitable military force, until she became United Earth, accepting the whole world problems and troubles as hers, then one day an Air Force war plane was jetting in the air on the alert, flying through the cloud, and all of a sudden, it crashed into an unknown space ship. When the wreckage from the crash hit the ground, and was investigated, there were enough evident from the wrecked space ship, proving that we were attacked by another existence from out of space.

These people looked like human beings with reptile type of complexions, which were bullet proof to an ordinary bullet. It would take an armor-piercing bullet to kill them. These creatures also had wings that fold into their backs, when they wanted to walk or run, and unfold when they wanted to fly. They didn't need oxygen to breath, unlike human beings, there was an organ of their bodies that produce oxygen, and they had discovered, that the flesh of human beings were delicious to eat, and now they want to fed on the flesh of human beings, as a mean for them to survive.

Ulrica was re-elected as not only as the president of the United States, but of United Earth without any opposing opponent throughout the world, because the threat of these creatures had the world looking forward for Ulrica to make the decision on how the world was going to deal with them. These reptiles looking people had zigzag teeth, and they were originally from the planet Mar.

A thousand years ago, a group of them found their way to the moon, and went inside the moon to live, increasing their population, until their food supply began to run low, and some years ago, they sent a group of exploders to Earth, to learn about our existence.

These alien exploders hid out in deep remote areas of this world, studying us human being, learning how intelligent we were with our technologies, scientific qualities, the invention of military weapon, and what interested them the most was the flesh of human beings was delicious enough to eat, bringing nutrient to their existences, and that is why they are planning on leaving from inside the moon, and conquer Earth, because they like eating us.

When these creatures first invaded the world, they went into the ground to do their research on the people of Earth, and during the conflict between obesity and other people, some of the fat people found with their bodies tore apart or half eaten, all weren't done by this series killer, taking his grudge out on fat people. It was these creatures feeding on them; also during the past history of missing people, these creatures ate some of them. There were videos found in this wrecked space ship, showing different creatures out in the woody areas feeding on people, those types of people who like camping out in the wood were eaten alive by these human reptiles.

Another thing was discovered about these creatures, was if one of them found a live human being his or her size, and it eats this person alive, this creature would take on the appearance of the person he or she has eaten without breathing.

Earth received a televised message through its satellite, showing millions of these human size creatures, young, middle age and old, flying out of caves like holes from the moon, coming toward Earth. The Declaration of War was passed by the politicians of Earth, and signed by President Ulrica D'Angelo- Wilson.

People of this world were being equipped with the type of uniforms and weapons to fight these creatures, and they were loading up on huge air crafts by the thousands, going into space to meet these invading creatures in the atmosphere, with the attempt to kill them all there, to prevent any more of them from reaching Earth. Some of the citizens of Earth thought the world was coming to an end, especially, if these creatures were coming here to feed on the flesh of them.

There was a law passed to check every human being living on earth to see whether he or she was breathing naturally, if not he or she was a creature, and will be killed, immediately. Ulrica was preparing to address the world with her speech on the invasion of these creatures. The night before her speech, I had a disturbing dream about this incident, and warn her about an assassinating attempt on her life.

During Ulrica's speech, addressing the world, she was seeking their approval to fire a nuclear attack on these creatures coming out of the moon, because a conventional war, the Earth couldn't win, and if we use nuclear weapons, there's a possibility the moon will be destroyed, taking away the nights, and the world will find it hard to sleep without the darkness of such existence, and it will also affect the tides of our water, because the moon has something to do with that.

As Ulrica was speaking, all kinds of reporters were there with all kinds of cameras, and I saw the type of camera that appeared in my dream. I shouted out gun! while drawing my weapon, firing it, as this camera person shot a bullet from the camera's Len. I had jumped in front of Ulrica. My bullet hit this assassinator in his head, but not until he had fired his camera gun, launching an armor-piercing bullet through my bullet proof vest, into my chest, and out of my back into Ulrica's breast, who was also wearing a bullet proof vest, under her dress. This armor-piercing bullet went through my body with enough force, sending me flying against Ulrica, knocking us both to the floor.

I could feel the burning painful hole through my chest, heart and back. I was laying backward on top of Ulrica's body, shriveling and shaking while gasping for air, death was on its way. Ulrica was holding me in her arms, crying out loud, "Oh, God, no, my husband is shot! Please rush him to the hospital." Two of Ulrica's security men removed me from Ulrica's hugging arms, and left me lying on the floor, and Ulrica screamed out loud, "Oh, no, please don't let my husband die!"

One of her security men replied, "Ms. President, the first gentleman is dead, the bullet went through his chest, taking a piece of his heart with it, through his back, and entered into your breast. He is dead, Ms. President, there is nothing we can do for him. We have to rush you to the hospital."

As they were removing Ulrica from the scene, she started, crying, hollering and screaming, "Oh, God, no, please don't take me away from my husband, I want to die here with him." Some other people in this area were looking at me with a sad expression on their faces, most of the ladies there were crying. They rushed Ulrica from the scene. The pain from my fatal bullet wound began to cease, and then I began to witness the most euphoric feeling of my existence.

Now, I know that dying is the best feeling a person can witness, until he or she stop breathing. Now I feel nothing, death has conquered my existence, all of a sudden, a bright glowing tunnel of light came down from the sky encircling my entire body, as I lay there with no feeling at all.

My body began to rise up in this tunnel of light. That when I started talking to God. "Oh, God Almighty, please, Lord Jesus, don't take me away from my wife and children. My family needs me, Lord. Life was good to me while I was living, but it wasn't always, peaches and cream, if you know what I mean, until I met Ulrica, God, my wife and children need me. I beg of you, Lord Jesus, to spare me of this deathful experience. I repent all of my sins, please give me another chance to live again."

All of a sudden, this bright tunnel of light disappeared, and I realized that I was alive above the cloud, falling down toward the ground, fear invaded my heart, and I started hollering out these words. "Oh, Lord, I'm still going to die, when I hit the ground." I was hollering and screaming, "Oh, God, please save me from this deadly event."

I was falling to the ground so fast, knowing that my body will burst on impact, and as I collided against the ground, I jumped up from my dreadful sleep with sweat of fear, popping from my body like a lawn sprinkler sprinkling water. I began to pray, thanking God that this was a dream, and I have another chance at life to live again.

This story tells how a person can live within a dream. That what make life so beautiful to some human beings, because they have the ability to dream. Reality can be full of misery, but a dream can bring some pleasure to such an existence, and as mysterious as some dreams can be, the phenomenon of it can enhance a person existence in reality.

Love and Understanding Is Happiness

The presence of a person
Can be eyes
Pleasing to see

To another individual
With a heartwarming feeling
To get better acquainted

With such a person's existence
There was an introduction
Of each other

Speaking words of encourage
To learn more
About one another

Through a conversation
They listen to what
Each other has to say

Ended up negotiating
On a date
In a compromising way

They found that
Each other's personality
Was interested to be near

Analyzing the thoughts
Each expresses with feeling
Of understanding the

Difference of agreement
After founding out
The like and dislike

Of him and her
They adjusted their lives
Styles in a way

He or she will appreciate
Now they are doing it again
Just like close friends

There to listen
When one is about
To make a decision

And need someone to discuss
The solution with
They became emotional interest

In each other's existence
Doing what it takes
To enhance him or herself

For the other person's sake
They fell in love
With each other that way

Getting intimately involved
Having control over
Each other's heart

Doing things together
Always makes them feel better
Like a child who has been away

From his or her mother
The happiness shows in their
Eyes when they see one another

This is the ingredient
Of being husband and wife
Partners of their house

Making decisions on how
They are going to
Live their lives

Together as spouse
Collaborating on
Their financial situation

Whether or not
They can afford
To have a child

Doing the things it takes
To make their child's life great
Rearing him or her

Up in a respectfully way
Whether it one, two children or more
A family life is to learn

As they grow old
Showing love and understanding
Each other individuality

Is the happiness
Between the existences
Of two human beings